The four of us started to skate, faster and faster. Soon we were catching up to the guys.

Then my friends let me go.

I was like that battery bunny. I kept going, and going . . .

And then I was crashing into . . . all of them. Two of them went down onto the ice and I landed on top of one.

Then someone else kind of wrapped his arms around my waist and lifted me up. "Didn't I tell you to be careful?" I looked over my shoulder and saw that it was Sean. His hands were warm and he wasn't even wearing gloves.

Good grief, I thought. It was almost worth falling again.

CATHERINE CLARK

Icing on the Lake

AVON BOOKS
An Imprint of HarperCollins *Publishers*

Chapter 1

Stop. Stop! I commanded my skates.

"Look out!" I cried, seconds before I nearly smashed into a group of boys. Instead, I opted just to fall onto the snowbank, my legs crumpling beneath me, landing on my hip and lurching backward. *Very smooth, Kirsten,* I thought. Could I go home now? I'd had about as much embarrassment as I could take for one morning.

"Come on, girls," one of the boys said as he skated over toward us.

"Sure, where are we going?" my friend Jones (whose real name is Bridget, but no one calls her that) said under her breath to me as she helped me up from the ice. "I think I could follow *him* just about anywhere."

I fought back a laugh. Jones was right:

Official Rink Guy, whoever he was, was extremely cute, but he also looked like steam might come out of his ears at any moment.

Then again, we were *all* sort of steamy, which sounds sexy, but wasn't, because it was only due to the fact that it was 12 degrees outside—and *everyone* steams in that cold. Dogs' breath can be seen from a mile away, especially when they're sled dogs running across the frozen tundra—

Okay, so this wasn't Alaska, and this wasn't the Iditarod—it was just Minneapolis, Minnesota, on your average late-December day.

And it was a gorgeously sunny day, which meant it was *extra* cold. We were at the park near my sister's house, which happens to have a huge cleared skating area, as well as a couple of enclosed rinks. The lake had some scattered ice fishing houses, which looked strange to me—the last time I was here, I'd hung out on the beach and built sandcastles with my nephew Brett.

The rink guy still stood there glaring at us with disapproval. He had a whistle on a chain around his neck, and he was wearing a red sports-team type jacket with the name Sean stitched on the front, sort of like a varsity letter jacket. Sean—I liked that name. He had blond hair, brown eyes, and was seriously tall. But then everyone looks taller on skates. Anyway, he didn't look cold in the twelve-degree, wind-chill-of-five weather. He wasn't even wearing a hat or gloves.

"Be a little more careful, okay? That's all I ask," he said.

"Careful? We are being extremely careful," Jones replied as she brushed snow off my back. (The good skaters *never* have snow on their backs.) "Have we killed anyone yet?"

"No, but there are lots of little kids skating here—I don't want anyone to get hurt," he said.

"But if the adults get hurt, *that's* okay?" Jones said.

He smiled, and his whole face went from semi-tough-looking to very-gorgeous. "You're funny. But no. That wouldn't be too cool, either. Just take it easy. Don't do anything crazy, okay?"

He shook his head and skated off to rejoin his friends, or should I say, co-skating-rink rule enforcers. They were circling the skating area as a group, as if they were the rink police of south Minneapolis, on the lookout for skating crimes. I kept my eyes trained on Sean for a lap. Watching someone that comfortable on his skates really impressed me. He was skating so fast, completely in control, and he looked good doing it, too. He had to be an awesome hockey player.

My friend Emma was a good skater, too, but me? Not so much. I was more into soccer and softball. When we went skating and played Crack the Whip, like today, I just held on for dear life and hoped for the best.

"He's very good-looking, but he needs to lighten up," Jones complained as she, too, watched the guys skating around. "Hasn't he ever seen people play Crack the Whip?"

"Maybe it's not a big thing here," I suggested. "Maybe there are different rink rules or something."

"Yeah, well, 'Crack the Whip' does sound a little . . . iffy. Doesn't it?" Jones asked.

"Iffy how?" I asked.

"A little sadistic. That's all I'm saying."

I punched Jones lightly on the arm. "You're

the only one who would think that."

"Thank you." She took a deep bow, which made her wobble a little on her skates. "Whoa. That's harder than it looks. End of the Non-Stars on Ice show."

"Look at Emma," I said. "Speaking of stars on ice."

She was doing a spin, and the guys that we were watching had stopped skating to watch *her*.

"She's taken!" Jones pretended to yell across the ice, her hand cupped around her mouth. Then she sighed. "It must be difficult to be gorgeous and talented."

"Let me tell you about it," I said.

"Ha!" She laughed.

We call our friend Emma "Emma Dilemma" because everything eventually becomes a giant problem with her—even the tiniest, most inconsequential things, like what to order for lunch or what shoes to wear. She's beautiful and sweet and has a tendency to be undecided, which is a bad combination because she always has some boyfriend or other pining for her while she goes out with another guy because she thinks she should give him a chance, too.

She constantly comes to her friends for advice. It can drive you nuts at times, but she makes up for it by being really nice and thoughtful. She never forgets important days for you, she's always bringing little gifts, and donating her slightly-used clothes and shoes (and boys) to charity—meaning me and Jones, because Crystal, who completes our group of four, has a serious boyfriend.

Crystal, meanwhile, was tilting her face to the sun, hoping to feel some warmth. Crystal had a gigantic winter coat that always made me think of Kenny on "South Park"—it's orange, with a big cone-like hood around her head that looks like an old diving helmet, only it has fur around the edges. Crystal and her family moved here from Colorado last year and she still hasn't adjusted to the low temps and the occasional four-day lack of sunshine.

My sister, Gretchen, was sitting on the bench beside the ice with her leg sticking straight out, looking as frozen as a fishstick.

I didn't know why she had come along with us to the lake, actually. I guess either she was still hanging on to the concept of being my big-sister chaperone, or she was sick of staying inside the house with a gigantic brace on her leg, or else she was hoping to meet a nice single guy who loved kids, which is what she's usually hoping to do.

Sometimes I really worry about my sister. Whenever I hear stories about girls buying wedding gowns and rings for themselves when they're not even dating someone, it kind of makes me think she might do something like that. She can be a little out there at times. Besides, she was so obsessed with the concept of marriage that she got married at twenty-one . . . and was divorced by twenty-three.

Maybe that was partly why my parents had jumped all over the idea of me coming to stay with her, so that I could check up on her and make sure she was doing all right. Since her divorce last year, she's been pretty down, which is completely understandable.

But I mean, it was her idea to separate from Luke. Doesn't that mean she should be getting over it faster?

Of course, there were a couple other reasons I was staying with her.

One, my nephew Brett, who's three years old and adorable—when he's not having a tantrum or pouring cold beverages down your back.

Two, their dog, Bear, who's one of those giant white Samoyeds and looks like a polar bear except that he moves a lot quicker than a bear.

(Then again, I've never seen a polar bear run. Maybe they can really book.)

And three, the fact my sister crashed while skiing and landed really badly and broke her right leg in several different places, which meant she couldn't really take care of either her dog or her child all that well because she couldn't drive, or walk. It happened when she came home for Christmas and she was really rather pathetic, her leg half reconstructed with pins and bolts, which is when we all hatched this plan for me to spend my January—and February, if necessary—in the Twin Cities. I was basically done with school and ready to graduate, except for an Independent Study in English—a writing project, which I could work on here as easily as at home. I needed to meet with my adviser now and then, and fill out some forms for graduation, but that was about it.

"Kirsten, we would really appreciate it if you could do something that's important for the whole family." My mom put it in these very serious, very guilt-inducing terms.

But the truth was, I didn't need that much convincing. Even though Gretchen and I had never been that close, because of the seven-year age difference between us, and the fact that she still treated me as if I were nine, instead of eighteen, I had always looked up to her, in some ways. And others, not so much.

There were tons of things I wanted to do here—go to museums, like the Minneapolis Institute of Arts and the Walker, and check out a play at the Guthrie Theater, and catch some sports events at the U or the Target or Xcel Centers. Of course, with Gretchen laid up, and me looking after a three year old, I probably wouldn't get to do any of those things, but they were on the list. I'd miss my friends, but it was only a month we were talking about.

Gretchen was so thrilled by the idea of me coming to stay with her for a month that she scared me. Was she that desperate for companionship that she'd take in "Cursed" Kirsten for a few weeks? (She'd nicknamed me that when she was twelve and thought it was hilarious. Now that she was twenty-four, apparently it still was.)

When I'd tried to convince her to let me stay with her two years ago, for my April vacation week, she'd done everything she could to talk me out of it. She'd gotten mad at me and Jones back when we were fourteen and we acted goofy at her wedding, and she'd never given me any credit for maturing beyond that.

Now there was this sudden interest in her taking me "under her wing." I'd never been under anyone's wing. I didn't know if I would like it. The position didn't exactly sound comfortable . . . for either one of us. I didn't understand why she saw me as some sort of project that needed work, like the way she went berserk with her home renovation and redecoration plans, but I could put up with it for a month if it helped *her*.

"Come on, Kirsten. Let's do it again!" Emma skated over and took my hand.

"We probably shouldn't. Those guys keep watching us," I said.

"They haven't really taken their eyes *off* us. Or you, anyway," Jones said to Emma with a smile.

"They want to watch us? Let's give them something to watch," she said with a grin. "Come on, Crystal!"

The four of us got into a line, and somehow I ended up on the end again. "Hey, no fair," I said as we started to skate, faster and faster. Soon we were catching up to the guys.

Then my friends let me go.

I was like that battery bunny. I kept going, and going . . .

And I couldn't stop. And then I was crashing into . . . all of them. Two of them went down onto the ice and I landed right on top of one.

"Are you okay?" one of them I'd fallen onto asked, his face turning red, and getting redder and redder the longer I stayed flattened on top of him.

Then someone else kind of wrapped his arms around my waist and lifted me up. "Didn't I tell you to be careful?" I looked over my shoulder and saw that it was Sean. His hands were warm as he touched my skin—my jacket was short and my shirt had come untucked from my low-rise jeans—and he wasn't even wearing gloves.

"S-sorry," I stammered, as he held onto me for a few seconds longer than necessary.

The boy I'd landed on top of—who'd valiantly tried to stop me—got to his feet and asked, "You okay?"

"Fine," I said. "Sorry. Really sorry about that."

He shrugged. "No problem." I watched as he skated away. He was nearly as good on his skates as Sean—who was still holding onto my arm. "Just don't let it happen again," Sean said, "or we'll have to show you how it's really done." He gave me a little squeeze as he pushed me toward my friends.

Good grief, I thought. It was almost worth falling again.

"Congratulations, one of them is still standing," Jones told me as I wobbly skated over to her.

Everyone was giggling and I couldn't help smiling, too.

"You know what? Let's go inside," Crystal

suggested. "Before they kick us out of the rink for good."

"Great idea," I said. "It'll be easier to kill you all when you're on solid ground."

"You don't want to kill us," Jones said. "Thanks to us you just met a completely adorable guy. Or four or five of them, actually."

"True. And thanks to you, they all know I'm a complete klutz. Cursed Kirsten strikes again."

We walked up the wooden ramp and steps into the park building to take off our skates, still laughing. A Girl Scout troop was selling hot chocolate while they took orders for cookies. We each got some and then went to sit by the window so we could check out the guys some more.

But all we could see was Gretchen glaring through the glass because we'd forgotten and left her outside with Brett. She didn't want to come in and be tempted to have a hot chocolate with whipped cream on top, never mind order twelve boxes of Girl Scout cookies. If I were on a diet I probably would have avoided them as well.

Gretchen was very skilled at dieting. She

did it a little too often, in my opinion, but when she was really into it she didn't even seem to be tempted by the stuff she couldn't have. She just stayed away. Period. It was funny because she couldn't do that with anything else in her life, like shoes, or new types of makeup.

Gretchen's breath sort of fogged up the glass as she knocked on the window. "Let's go," she mouthed.

"Five minutes," I mouthed back, pointing to my watch. If I let her start bossing me around too much on Day One, I'd be doomed.

"God, your sister hasn't changed a bit," Jones commented.

"What? I think she's nice," Emma said.

"She is nice. Very nice," I said in her defense. "When she wants to be." I did feel sorry for her. Her leg was probably freezing back into the wrong angles. It might never heal, in this climate.

"It's just that she's starting a diet, and she's pretty grumpy right now," I explained. "Or extra grumpy, anyway."

"Why would she go on a diet? She looks fine. Anyway, that's dumb. She should just exercise more," Crystal said.

"Hello? Broken leg?" Jones reminded her. "What's she going to do, jog around the lake on one leg?"

"Oh." Crystal snapped her fingers. "Right."

"And whatever you do, don't get into it with her, don't give her any advice," I told everyone. "She'll bite your head off."

"That hungry, huh?"

"Yeah. Besides, she's always been kind of a perfectionist," I explained. "So the fact everything now completely sort of sucks . . . I guess it's getting to her. She had to make a New Year's resolution, and, being a perfectionist, she had to start *before* New Year's."

"You know what? I really *hate* New Year's resolutions," Jones said.

"Why?" Crystal asked.

"Because, people make them, they get really intense about them, they're so boring because that's all they talk about, on and on about how they're going to really do it this time, and then they're unhappy when they can't stick to them two weeks later."

"Um . . . what about good intentions?" Emma

asked. "Any credit for those?"

Jones shook her head.

"I don't know, I think resolutions can be kind of cool," I said. "Stepping back and looking at your life and deciding what you want to do, or change." I'd always admired people who could do that—decide to run a marathon, or volunteer more, or quit smoking or some other equally bad and addictive habit.

Of course, when I was a kid and I tried to give up gummy bears for a month, I'd failed miserably. When I tried to train to run a marathon in Duluth with my dad last year, I ended up running a 5K instead. And my last volunteer assignment? Well, I think coming here to take care of Brett was the only thing even close to qualifying.

"Hello. Rink police at twelve o'clock," Jones said under her breath.

The guys I'd plowed into—two of them with the same official-looking team jacket—came into the shelter. They pushed and shoved each other on their way over to get hot chocolate, still wearing their skates but with skate guards on. They nearly flattened a small child against the wall, and they had the nerve to complain about me?

As we eyed them over our hot cocoa, we all immediately, without discussing it, started talking a bit more loudly about where we were going for lunch. Yeah, we can be kind of immature when we want to be.

I thought I saw Sean look over at me a few times, but by the time I'd glance over, he was always looking away. We were finally about to make genuine eye contact when Jones said, "Let's make an exit."

"Right," I said quickly. No point getting carried away. After all, hadn't I had enough contact with the guy already today?

Emma, Jones and Crystal got into Emma's Explorer to follow us, while I walked to the minivan to drop off Gretchen and Brett before the girls and I headed out for our farewell New Year's lunch and celebration. I walked beside the lake and noticed the group of guys had come back onto the ice and were buzzing around, racing each other.

"Hey! Wait up!"

I turned around and saw one of the guys

from the crash incident. He was the one I'd sort of landed on top of when I fell, the one who had asked if I was okay.

When he stopped, he sprayed me with ice shavings. He had to have been practicing that stop since birth to be that good at it. Like, you could have taken the shavings and sprinkled them on a gourmet dessert, that's how good and fine and delicate they were.

"You lost your hat," he said.

"I did?" I laughed, embarrassed, as I reached up to my head to confirm that, yes, I had completely lost my hat at some point. And also to confirm that, yes, despite the fact I'd lost my hat a while ago, I still had really bad hat hair. I think some of my hair was floating straight up in the air from static. "Yes. I guess I did," I said.

I reached for the hat, but before I could grab it from him he pulled it over my head, down to my ears, like a sock. I felt like a two-year-old being dressed by my mom.

"You lost it out on the ice, when you fell," he said.

I felt my face turning bright red. "Thanks for

bringing it to me. I would have really missed it tomorrow."

"Better luck next time," he said.

"Huh?"

"With Crack the Whip. The first thing you learn when you're playing Crack the Whip is to make sure you're not on the end. But if you are, hang on, no matter what."

"Gee. Thanks. I'll try to remember that," I said.

His smile vanished. "Just trying to help."

Why, Kirsten? I asked myself as I adjusted my hat and watched him skate away from me. Why did you just act like that?

Chapter 2

My friends and I went over to Noodles & Co. in Highland Park for our goodbye lunch. It's a chain restaurant, but it's still one of our favorite places in St. Paul because no matter what time we go, there always seems to be a big crowd of people our age, so it's cool to hang out there.

After lunch, Crystal, Emma and Jones were driving home, so they could be there for New Year's Eve. They had big plans. I did not.

"So, I am going to see you guys soon, right?" I asked after our dishes were delivered to the table and we started to eat. "You're coming for Winter Carnival at the end of the month. Promise me." I savored a bit of the spicy Thai noodles I'd ordered.

"And we'll show up other times, too," Emma said. "When you least expect it."

"Good, because I think I'm going to be really lonely," I said.

"Lonely? No way. We won't strand you here," Jones said. "I mean, what are you going to do? What are *we* going to do at home without you?"

"Go to school every day," I reminded her.

Jones sighed. "I hate you for being smart," she said. "I do. Except that when you become a rich and successful lawyer or television producer or screenwriter or whatever, you'll invite me over to swim in your full-length pool." She tapped my bowl with her fork. "You will invite me. Right?"

"Definitely," I said.

"If I were you, Kirsten? I'd go back to that skating rink at the lake every day," Emma said. "Did you *see* how many cute guys were there?"

"Kirsten, I know! You could take skating lessons there!" Crystal cried. "Then you'd meet tons of—"

"Girls, six-year-old girls," I interrupted her. "With wobbly ankles."

"Oh." Crystal's nose twitched, a little like a rabbit's. "Kids. Yeah. Probably."

"Just once I'd like to meet a guy with wobbly ankles. He'd need to lean on me. A ton," I said. "He'd be an even worse skater than me and I'd hold him up around the rink and laugh at him when he fell down."

"Somehow that doesn't sound like the kind of guy we'd fall for," Emma said.

"But . . . wait a second. Back to this skating class idea." Emma tapped her chopsticks against her bowl of mac and cheese. She insisted on using chopsticks every time we ate here, no matter what type of noodles she ordered and no matter how difficult they were to pick up. "I think we're onto something. Because I wonder who would be *teaching* the class. Maybe one of those hotties on the skating squad from today."

"What was the deal with those rink police guys?" Jones complained. "Some people should not be allowed to have power. They completely let it go to their head."

I smiled, thinking of the way the one guy had pulled my hat over my ears. Maybe he was a bit obnoxious, but he was cute, too. I quickly told everyone the story, pointing out he couldn't be that terrible of a person, since he bothered to find me to return my hat.

Then again, he hadn't been all that suave about it, had he. Especially not after he'd tried to be nice and I'd been rude in return.

"He brought your hat back? Cool. That means he likes you," Emma said.

"No, I don't think so," I said. At least, not so much anymore.

"Yes, of course," she said. "Otherwise, why would he bother? He was looking for an excuse to talk to you."

"Or to harass me," I said. "Come to think of it, if he really liked me, he wouldn't have made fun of me. *And*, he would have kept the hat in the Lost & Found, so I'd have to come back and he could see me again."

"Well, drop your hat again the next time you go skating at the lake with Brett. Just in case he wants to keep it. As ransom," Emma said with a grin.

Jones rolled her eyes. "Guys don't do that."

"Can it hurt to try?" Crystal wondered. "The dude was cute. Leave your phone number inside the hat next time, maybe."

"Oh, yeah. *Sew* it in," Jones said, rolling her eyes.

"I think actually it would be a knitting project," I told her. "And I can't knit, so don't worry. Anyway, I'll see if he's around the next time I go."

"Go tomorrow," Emma urged. "Or maybe tonight. Skating on New Year's Eve's so romantic."

More romantic than my current New Year's Eve plans, anyway, I thought. Emma and Crystal both had plans to go out with their boyfriends that night. Jones was going to a big party with them, too. I'd be sitting around home with Gretchen and Brett.

Just once I wanted to have romantic New Year's Eve plans. Was that so much to ask?

"I know you hate New Year's resolutions, Jones. But I was thinking, if we all wrote something down, it would be a great start to my writing project. You know, for my Independent Study—it's going to be a collection of different forms of writing." I was compiling poems, stories, and various fragments of writing: mine, as well as famous people's, as well as not-so-famous people's (my friends). I had told my English teacher and project adviser, Mrs. McCutcheon, that I'd study how editors decided to do anthologies by deciding what to put in and what to keep out. The theme of the project was "Life & Times: Mine and Others."

"You guys can help me kick it off. We can check in later with a progress report—just a sentence or two, no big deal. Write down a goal, a wish . . . anything." I got a small, striped notebook out of my bag along with a pen and gently pushed it to the center of the table.

"Why do we have to have *goals*?" Jones complained. "Can't we just exist? Isn't that hard enough in January?"

"Hey, I'm the one who hates winter. You're not allowed to," Crystal said.

"Maybe your goal for the new year could be not to hate winter so much, Crystal," Emma suggested. "You could buy a new, warmer coat. And get out in the cold and just—"

"Embrace it? You weren't going to say 'embrace it,' were you?" Jones asked her.

I laughed. "You know how she hates that phrase."

"Unless the word *embrace* is connected to the words *Topher Grace*, then yeah, I do." She sipped her soda. "Embrace Topher Grace. It's a mini-poem. Hey, Kirsten, put that down in your book."

"No, *you* do it." I pushed the notebook toward her plate.

I wouldn't be surprised if she took up a few pages; Jones's obsession with the actor was well-documented. Her normally cool and detached attitude didn't apply where he was concerned. She had a "Toph-oto" Album, full of pictures of him. She'd even tried to convince her ex-boyfriend, Chris, to go by the name "Topher" instead. The fact that he hadn't didn't make her break up with him, but it didn't help his cause, either. She actually had never forgiven him for saying that Topher was "just sort of okay" in *Win a Date with Tad Hamilton*.

"Since you're so interested in goals, Kirsten, you know what your goal for the next month should be?" Emma asked.

"Get along with my sister, even when she's

being a pain?" I asked. That sounded like a worthy aspiration. Gretchen had this thing where she treated me like she was my mother sometimes. She didn't see it, whenever I called her on it, but trust me—it was there.

"No. Actually, I say *don't* make a huge effort to get along with her. You're doing her a huge favor by staying here and helping her with Brett, and if she's so self-centered that she can't appreciate it—"

"I know, I know. Look, things with my sister will be fine." I stood up and went to refill my cola. I knew my friends were only trying to be supportive, but somehow there's something different about *me* dissing my sister and other people doing it. Like, if I joked about how horrible she was, that was one thing. But if someone else commented on it, I felt the need to defend her, like she was a lion in my pride. Not that I know much about lions. Or pride, after the way I'd fallen ten times that morning.

I sat back down at the table, resolved to change the subject if necessary.

"We've talked it over and we decided we're going to give you a task," Crystal said.

"Darn it." I snapped my fingers. "I was at the pop machine too long, wasn't I?"

"You like New Year's resolutions, right? You said so." Emma smiled at me.

I started to get that sinking feeling you get when you know your friends are about to dare you. "Okay . . ." I said slowly.

"So, starting tomorrow, you're going back to that lake. You're—"

"Learning how to skate better, first of all," Jones said. "Or not, because you did meet lots of guys today when you knocked them down. Anyway, we want you to meet a guy there at the rink. Preferably one with several good-looking friends—"

"One of whom bears an uncanny resemblance to Topher Grace, so that I can hook you up, too?" I interrupted.

"Well. That wouldn't hurt your case any." Jones grinned at me.

"I know I said I liked resolutions, but I was thinking more along the lines of 'Be more outgoing in the new year.' How about if I just say something like, 'I'll be more outgoing'?" I offered.

"That's nice. That's wonderful," Emma said. "And best of all, it'll help you meet a guy you can invite to come with us on Groundhog Getaway."

"No," I said. "Impossible."

"It's not impossible," Emma said. "Don't be ridiculous. You have a month."

Groundhog Getaway was a weekend trip to a cabin resort, and it was supposed to be our first major "adult" trip. Our parents had given us the okay to go there for a long weekend, right around Valentine's Day.

But, natural procrastinators that we all were, we hadn't gotten around to booking the reservation until too late, and by the time we got around to it, the weekend closest to Valentine's Day was full . . . and the only weekend even remotely close that was available was Groundhog Day.

You have to admit it wasn't *quite* as romantic-sounding.

We'd tried to come up with a cute name for it, like Hibernation Weekend, or Snuggle Down Weekend. So far, it was still being referred to as Groundhog Getaway. And me bringing someone was still impossible.

"You're giving me a month to meet a guy and get to know him well enough to invite him on a weekend trip," I said to Emma. "Are you insane?"

"Yes, she is, but that's not the issue," Jones said. "The issue is that we think you're great, and you deserve a romantic weekend just like the rest of us."

"Oh, really? That's sweet, but who are *you* bringing?" I asked her. As far as I knew—and I knew pretty much everything about Jones— she didn't have a boyfriend, either. Neither of us had any prospects, exactly.

"Well. I'm not sure yet," she said. "If nothing else turns up? I'll ask Chris."

"You dumped him," I reminded Jones.

"Yeah, but he's a good skier and he knows how to build a fire. He'd be fun to have along."

"So you're inviting him because he's a Boy Scout, basically," Crystal observed.

"*Was* a Boy Scout," Jones said. "He didn't make eagle. I think he got stuck at like pigeon scout."

We were all laughing, so I decided not to tell her how mean that would be, to invite a guy who was still basically in love with her. "Okay," I said. "So you want me to find someone to invite. Well, that, uh, begs the question. Does inviting someone count, or do they actually have to show up with luggage and stick around for the weekend?"

"Ooh . . . *they*? You're bringing more than one guy now?" Jones teased me. "Hot!"

"Ha ha. Very funny. I'll be lucky if I bring my nephew and the dog," I said.

"Oh, please. It's not like you've even asked anyone," Crystal said. "There are tons of guys at school who'd jump at the chance to spend the weekend with you."

"Okay, but I'm not even going to be *home* before Groundhog Getaway," I said.

"Which is why you can find a guy here," Emma argued. "It's not going to be a problem."

"Yeah. Right." I've never had a real, or real serious anyway, boyfriend.

I did go out with this guy Tyler last year for a few weeks, but then he fell for Emma.

Everyone acts like it's no big deal that I haven't dated much, and it isn't, I guess. Except that at times you do feel a little left out, and a little . . . old-maid-ish.

First it was that my parents were being super protective, not letting me date until I was sixteen because my sister was a bit, well, promiscuous.

Well, that backfired on them, now, didn't it? Seeing as how they drove away any potential boys in the surrounding area by forcing me to tell them, "No, thank you, I can't, my parents won't let me." Some boys asked me once or twice, and then gave up for good. Other boys met my father when he came to pick me up after a group date and realized he is a very large, very strong, ex-football-playing-lineman-tackle. And they knew my mother from her showing up at school sporting events, like my soccer games, and screaming like crazy until you thought, well, maybe she *is* crazy.

You can't escape your family in a small town. I was doomed to remain a spinster until at least twenty-five, unless I got out of Cloquet.

Well, here I was, in the Cities for the next month. Leave it to me to antagonize the first boys I saw.

"You know, if you don't find someone on

your own, we'll invite someone for you," Emma said.

"Yes, if you refuse to come up with a date, one will be provided for you," Jones said. "And we all have really terrible taste in guys, so you'd better pick for yourself."

I laughed.

"You're not going to have a problem meeting guys here," Emma said. "All you need to do is find your inner flirt."

"Inner what?" I asked.

"I saw a TV show about it," Emma said.

"Well, then, it *has* to be true." Jones rolled her eyes.

"Let's get in touch with our inner presents," Crystal said, lifting a bag onto the table. "You guys ready for gifts or what?"

The four of us have a tradition of giving New Year's gifts instead of holiday ones. That way we have something to look forward to after the big celebrations are all over. And, we can shop for more things on sale, and therefore get each other more presents.

The first gift I opened was a striped scarf from Emma. It matched my pink and orange puffy down jacket perfectly. "Maybe you could drop that at the rink, too," she suggested.

"Yeah, just leave random items of clothing there. See what happens," Jones added.

I lashed her with the scarf. "Shame on you. I'm not going to disrobe on an icy lake."

"Maybe not, but you'd find a date really fast if you did!" Jones said, and we were all laughing again.

That night, just before midnight, I made a pact with a fake fire.

I was staring at the dancing flames in the fireplace, and because I could see my reflection in the glass, flames appeared to be coming out of my head. I looked a bit possessed.

I was thinking: I resolve that next year, when New Year's rolls around, I'll have someone special to celebrate it with. Just once it would be great to go out on a fancy, expensive, special date with someone I really cared about. Who also happened to be very good-looking.

This year, Gretchen and I were watching the giant crystal ball preparing to drop in New York's Times Square. For a few reasons, I felt really excited about the new year. So many things could change—they *would* change, whether I wanted them to or not. I'd be spending half the summer working in a program for kids in Duluth and the other half on a trip to England with my high school English club.

"To getting out of high school this year," I said, raising my glass.

"To getting out of this cast this year." Gretchen clinked her glass against mine, then took a sip of the sparkling apple juice we were drinking instead of champagne. She had this rule about not having alcohol in the house when I was around, which I could have told her was completely unnecessary. I'm enough of a klutz without adding something else into the mix.

"To finding the perfect pair of shoes at Nordstrom on sale," Gretchen said.

"To world peace," I said.

My sister and I are similar in some ways . . . and others, not so much. We look alike, and yet we don't. We're both about 5'8", and we both could have the same blond hair, only she bleaches and highlights her hair so that it's very California. She gets her nails done weekly. She tans. She knows how to put makeup on perfectly so that it looks like she's only wearing a little.

My hair is its natural color. I wear a tiny bit of mascara and that's about it. I paint my own nails—fingers in winter, toes in summer.

"To losing ten pounds by February second, so no one sees *my* shadow," Gretchen proclaimed.

I smiled uneasily—February second. Groundhog Getaway Day.

"Come on!" Gretchen held her glass toward mine. "Okay, how about this one? To both of us meeting new guys this year and falling in love."

I raised my eyebrow. "Really? You're ready for that?"

"I've been dating plenty since the divorce."

"I know, but nobody serious. All really superficial," I said, thinking, *Kind of like you can be at times*. "Right?"

"True. But sometimes you look at me like I'm over the hill. I'm only twenty-four. So I made a bad choice the first time around, that doesn't mean, like, my romantic life is over," she said.

"To me the real question is, are *you* ready for meeting a new guy?"

"What? Of course I am. What do you mean?"

"Come on, Kirsten. You've been dragging your feet ever since things didn't work out with that Roger guy."

"Roger?" I asked.

"Wasn't it Roger?" she said.

"No, no Roger. Maybe you're thinking of the town. Rogers? Out near Plymouth?"

"Okay, so it wasn't Roger, you don't have to get snippy about it." She took a sip of the sparkling cider. "Richard then. That Richard guy."

I shook my head. "Still no." As I said earlier, we hadn't been all that close lately.

"Give me a clue," she pleaded.

"His name starts with a T."

"I've got it!" she cried. "His name was Taylor."

"Tyler," I said.

"Tinker tailor soldier spy. Whatever," she said with a wave of her hand. "I've forgotten him already, and you should, too."

"You didn't even know him."

"True. I didn't have much to go on except

Mom's stories," Gretchen said.

"I can imagine," I said. "Those must have been good."

"Good and boring, you mean. Yeah. But you're not still hung up on him, are you?" she asked.

"No! I'm actually really glad we broke up. I mean, it would have been better if it hadn't happened at *prom*, in front of the entire junior class, and it would have been better if it hadn't involved one of my best friends . . ."

Tyler had actually broken up with me because he thought he had a chance with Emma, because he was completely infatuated with Emma.

I didn't hold it against her. We both kind of enjoyed watching him make a fool out of himself. Well, she probably enjoyed it more than me, but still. Our friendship was stronger than Tyler.

"That did really suck, didn't it? Hmm. You don't want to date anyone else, though?" she asked. "No cuties in your class?"

"Cuties?" I wrinkled my nose.

"Cuties, hotties, dudes. Whatever," she said. "Isn't there anyone at home that you like?"

"No, not really. There aren't that many guys I'd want to date. And the ones I do like, usually like Emma first. Or . . . eventually."

"Yeah. I had a friend like that, too."

"You did?"

Gretchen nodded. "Her name was Ashley."

"Her name's not still Ashley?" I said.

She glared at me. "You're such a smart ass. No wonder you don't have a boyfriend."

"Hey! That's not fair."

"Sorry. All I was trying to say is that maybe we have more in common than you think. I mean, there's a lot you don't know about me. When I was in high school, you were, like, ten."

"True," I agreed.

"And, being ten, you weren't mature enough for me to talk to about things like boys. I wasn't about to tell you all the things that were going on at school."

"Not to mention the fact that you hated all of us back then, when I was ten. Actually, also when I was eleven, twelve, thirteen . . ."

"I didn't *hate* you."

"You didn't like us much, though."

"Sure I did!" Gretchen said. "I was a lot older

than you, that's all."

"Uh huh," I said, feeling a bit skeptical about this.

"I just . . . I needed to get away. Mom didn't quite understand who I was. Not that she does now, mind you, but she has a better idea. We have a better relationship." She shrugged. "You know what I mean, right?"

"I think so," I said. Was it that hard to understand who Gretchen was, though? She made it sound like she was a deep, intense, nuclear physicist. She liked shopping and clothes. Her number-one interest was looking good. It didn't go much beyond that, as far as I knew. But maybe now Gretchen and I could spend some time together and get to know each other as adults. If she'd treat me like an adult, which seemed doubtful.

"Time for me to go to sleep," she said, yawning.

"Don't yawn, you'll make me yawn." I took one of her arms and gently helped her get up from the sofa.

"Happy New Year!" she said and she gave me a little hug. "And good night!"

"I'd better take Bear outside for his first walk of the year before I turn in," I said.

"You can just let him out front, you know—he'll stay in the yard."

"No, that's okay. I actually really like walking in the snow," I said.

I grabbed Bear's leash and we went outside. Light snow was falling—it was supposed to snow overnight. There were already a couple of inches on the ground, which made the sky seem brighter. I started walking down the sidewalk, enjoying the cool flakes falling and melting on my face. It was one of those times when you feel like you're in control, and you just know that whatever you think can happen and come true. So I thought: *Maybe this was going to be My Year*. It was starting differently than the others. I could put the negative things behind me. They were so last year now—for real.

Chapter 3

I love waking up on snowy mornings—even if it's to the sound of a very loud snowplow scraping the street. I love the quiet, insulated feeling that settles over the world when it's snow-covered.

I sat up in bed and peeked out the window. Snow covered the trees. The mailboxes. The fence. The cars. The window boxes. The steps. Which made me think: *Ugh, I'll have to go out and start shoveling soon.* Gretchen wasn't going to be able to handle it, and Brett was a little on the small and short side to help out.

I wondered if Gretchen had a snowblower. Not that I knew how to use one, but I could learn. Then again, her ex-husband Luke would surely have gotten it in the divorce settlement.

He loved using that thing. Like my dad—he can't wait until it snows so that he can run the snowblower.

But the sun wasn't even up yet, and I wasn't going out there to shovel until it rose. I'd have some coffee and let the temperature warm up a little first.

As if it would.

I got the coffeemaker started and sat down on the sofa to read.

Scrape. Scrape.

What was that sound? I looked out the window and saw someone shoveling our driveway in front of the garage. *Are you kidding me?* I thought. *Gretchen has a snow shovel guy?*

Whoever he was, he was kind of hunky. I felt a little guilty as I sat on the sofa, indoors, completely toasty warm, watching someone else shovel. But if Gretchen had hired someone, then she didn't really need me to do it, did she?

Bear was whining loudly and pawing at me. He probably needed to go out. I thought about what Gretchen had said: I could just let Bear out in the yard. I'd have to be sneaky about it, so that shovel guy didn't see me in my pajamas.

As I slowly pulled the front door open wide enough for Bear to fit through, the first thing he did was run straight for the guy. He jumped on him, barking.

"Bear, stop!" I said. "Bear, come back!" I stepped out onto the front stoop, just in time to see Bear lick the guy's face.

He turned to me as Bear dropped to his feet and rubbed Bear behind the ears. "It's okay," he said. "Bear knows me—don't worry."

Not only does Bear know you, I thought as I watched him pet Bear, *I know you!* He was wearing his letter jacket again, so just in case I'd forgotten his name, which I hadn't, it was there to remind me: Sean.

"You look kind of familiar," I said casually. I didn't really want to refresh his memory, about the skating wipeouts. So I said, vaguely, "I've seen you down at the lake. Maybe."

"Oh, yeah?" He stood up and looked at me. "Yeah, of course. Yesterday. So . . . wait. You live here now? Or just visiting for the holidays?"

"Visiting," I said. "But I'm staying for a month or two," I added quickly, so he'd know that I'd be around. "Maybe more. So, do you like . . . are you hired by the neighborhood or the city or something?"

He laughed. "No, not exactly. I have a couple of part-time jobs, that's all. The rink, plus snow removal."

"You know? I didn't know Bear was such a good, ah, watch dog," I said awkwardly. And then I kind of realized what I'd done. I'd run outside in my pajamas, my hair was tied up loosely, and I had less than no makeup on. "So. Ah. Well." I looked down at my slippers. "Good shoveling," I said, nodding in appreciation.

He just stood there, frozen in action, shovel poised in mid-air. Staring at me. Completely speechless. And I thought, *Well, I can't really blame him.* He was here to shovel, not to look at someone who'd just rolled out of bed and probably had sheet-crease-face. Happy New Year, Cursed Kirsten.

I wrapped my arms around my chest, for obvious reasons. "Should we go in?" I asked.

"You probably should," he said.

"Come on, Bear!" I called, but of course he didn't come, he was too busy romping around the yard. I headed for the door anyway. I had to at least go put on some regular clothes, even if Sean would be gone by the time I did.

I rattled the door knob. Nothing. It was locked. I was locked out. And I was the only one awake so far.

"She keeps an extra key over here."

Sean's voice startled me. He was walking over to the porch swing. He reached underneath and picked up a fake rock.

"How well do you know my sister?" I asked.

"Well enough not to expect the key to actually be here," he said.

We both laughed.

"She must have used it and forgot to put it back," he said.

"Typical, really. She's been disorganized since birth," I told him.

"Really?"

"Yeah. She could never keep track of her bottle. Stuff like that." Why did I say that? I could have kicked myself, but then he'd see me kicking myself and that would be even more embarrassing than what I just said.

"But you're the younger sister . . . right?" he asked.

"Right," I said. "By, like . . . a lot. Seven years younger."

"So how would you know if she lost track of stuff since she was a baby?" he asked, still not getting it. "You were, uh . . ."

"Not even thought of at that point. I realize that. I was just joking."

"Oh." And then he grinned, giving me that killer smile of his again. "You're funny," he said.

Hilarious, I thought. If my friends could see me now.

I went over to pound on the front door while he cleared the side of the driveway, but nobody answered it. Then I leaned over and knocked gently on the living room's picture window. I knew Gretchen was still in bed, but I thought I saw Brett sprint past a couple of times, only he was so fast and little it was hard to tell with the sun coming up reflecting in the picture window. He usually woke up early so that he could watch the Koala Brothers on TV. Couldn't he be a good nephew and come save me?

I turned around and saw Bear romping across the yard, snow up to his torso. Watching Bear try to run through the snow, leaping and diving and burying his nose in it like a pig rooting for truffles, was hilarious. "Oh my gosh. He's completely buried," I said. "The snow's all the way up to his armpits."

"Armpits?" Sean said.

"Legpits, then?" I said. "What do you call them?"

"*Leg*pits?" Sean and I both began to laugh. Bear apparently wanted to join in, so he started barking. For some reason that made Brett finally notice us out there.

"Sean!" Brett cried as he pulled the front door open. "Sean, come in, come in! Come in *now*."

"Hey, kiddo!" Sean called back to him.

Thank you, Brett, I thought. I owed him, big-time. I was burying myself out there. Up to *my* armpits.

I looked over at Sean and smiled awkwardly. I wasn't sure what to do next. Summon your inner flirt, I heard Emma saying. "Hey. *Do* you want to come in for a second?" I blurted. "And see Brett? Plus, I think the coffee was almost finished brewing when I ran out the door. If you drink coffee. If you don't then that probably doesn't sound very good."

He looked at me as if I were completely nuts, as if everyone knew that you didn't invite the hired snow removal guy in for coffee, even if you did know his name because it was sewn into his jacket, and even if he did seem to know your nephew. He still didn't actually know *me*.

"I just thought . . . maybe you're cold. But you know, you're probably not, you're used to this kind of thing, plus you're active, plus you're not wearing, ah, PJ's—I mean, not that you're naked, because you are clothed, in fact—" *Oh God, did I just use the word "naked" in front of a cute guy?*

"Sure. I can come in for a few minutes," he said. "I always do your house last, 'cause it's on my way home."

"Oh really?" *And where would that home be?* "Well, great."

"I'll just finish up out here and then I'll be in," he said.

"Great!" I said. "I mean, uh, sounds good." I

quickly went inside, filled two mugs with coffee in the kitchen, then went back to the living room and managed to cover myself with one of Gretchen's fluffiest fleece throws before Sean walked in.

He took off his jacket, revealing a thick blue wool sweater with little white flecks on it, one of those expensive, classic Norwegian ski sweaters. Except it looked a little older and tattered, as if it had been passed down through the generations, which made it even more cool.

Most people don't really look that good when they take off their hat, but he really really did. His hair was sort of flattened and mashed and static-crazy, and he still looked great. His hair was the color of light wood, pine maybe. I think it was the way he was sitting near the stacked wood beside the fireplace.

My sister keeps cut logs of wood piled there, but it's purely decorative. She has a gas-insert fireplace, the kind you turn on with a remote control. It may not be as romantic as a real fireplace, but it's warm and very easy to use. Still, all her little decorations around the mantel, and the fake fire screen, are kind of ridiculous. She has a flair for home decoration. It's from watching too much HGTV.

I leaned over, managing to keep myself completely covered by the blanket, and flicked on the fire. Then we just glanced at each other and both sipped our coffee.

Where had Brett gone all of a sudden? He wasn't supposed to go back to bed. He was supposed to provide an amusing distraction.

"So. How much snow *did* we get?" I asked.

"I'd say about half a foot. Not bad." Sean nodded. "Do you cross-country ski?"

"Oh, yeah," I said. "I don't think I brought my skis, though. Shoot. Well, maybe I can borrow Gretchen's. So, are they building an ice palace for Winter Carnival this year?" I asked.

"No, I don't think so," he said. "I'm not totally sure though."

There was small talk, and then there was miniature talk.

"So, how often do you work down at the lake?"

"A few days a week. I mean, weekends for sure. Then some nights." He took a sip of coffee. "Why? Did you want to know when you should come down and single-handedly wipe out some more skaters?"

"I'm not that bad!"

"No. You're worse."

"Ha. Very funny," I said. "So okay, I'm no Sasha Cohen, but I can at least stay upright."

"Most of the time," he said.

I smiled. "Well, you know, the thing about Crack the Whip . . ."

"What?" he asked, giving me a confused look.

Oops. That must have been the other guy I sort of met yesterday, the one who brought back my hat. "Well, you just, you know, it's hard to stay upright when you're at the end of the line. And I haven't gone skating very much lately. You know, you get rusty." Or at least . . . your skate blades do. I smiled nervously.

"So you should skate a lot while you're here," he said.

"Yeah?" I asked, probably sounding a little too eager. "I mean . . . yeah. I will. Good to get Brett out of the house and all."

"You're here to look after Brett?" he asked.

I nodded. "And my sister. So, speaking of

skating. This is probably an obvious question, but you play hockey, right?"

"Yup."

"Cool. Well, maybe I can come to one of your games while I'm here." Then I coughed, realizing what a blatant invitation I'd just issued for myself. "I mean, I'm looking for stuff to do with Brett. He likes sports."

"Right. You know, I could try to teach him a few things. Even if he is named after a Green Bay Packer."

"That was his dad's idea. He's from Hudson."

"Yeah, I know Luke. He's a nice guy."

"He is," I agreed. "So, would you like some more coff—"

"*Sean?* What are you doing here?" Gretchen limped into the room, wearing a terrycloth robe over her sleepwear.

"Having some coffee and talking to your sister." He turned to me. "I didn't get your name."

"Kirsten," I said.

"Did you just get up, Kirsten?" Gretchen stared at me as if I had colored my hair green, or gotten a strange piercing. "Why are you in your *PJs*?" she said in a disapproving tone.

"Look, I didn't plan on going outside. Then I got locked out," I said. "It's a long story."

"More like the same old story." Gretchen laughed. "When she was little, Kirsten was always running around in her PJs."

Oh no you don't, I thought. *You are not about to tell an embarrassing story on me.*

But she was, of course.

"Kirsten even went to school in her PJs once. The school called and they were like, hello? Your daughter is wearing Care Bear footies."

Sean laughed.

"But that was *last* year," I joked. "I got sick of Care Bears."

Sean just looked at me and didn't seem to get it. Then he got to his feet. "I'd better get going. Nice to meet you, Kirsten. See you around, okay?"

"Definitely," I said. "Thanks for, ah, the coffee."

"You made the coffee."

"Having coffee, I meant. And the shoveling," I said. "Good work, excellent work."

"Well, have a good day, okay? See you later."

As Sean went out, Bear came running into the house. He stopped in the front entryway and shook his fur, sending ice and snow flying everywhere.

"Kirsten, could you grab a towel and get some of that cleaned up?" Gretchen asked.

After I closed the door, I turned around to face her. "Sure. But did you have to tell him that bit about the PJs?"

"That's nothing," she said. "Couldn't you have warned me that we had a guest, so that I didn't come out of my bedroom wearing a *robe*?"

"He's like . . . seven years younger than you are," I said.

"So what? That doesn't mean I want to look horrible when I see him. I could kill you."

Likewise, I thought. "If you're that concerned about a teenaged boy liking the way you look . . . I don't know, Gretch."

"Well, obviously *you're* not concerned," she replied.

"What's that supposed to mean?"

Gretchen made a sweeping motion to indicate my outfit of flannel.

"It's not my fault," I said. "Bear's the one who bolted and jumped all over Sean. I wasn't *planning* to run outside wearing this."

"You should get dressed as soon as you get up," Gretchen said. "You should brush your hair and get your makeup on."

"It was seven in the morning! And I didn't know you had hired a . . . a . . . shovel boy."

"Shovel boy?"

"You know what I mean. Besides, I don't really wear much makeup."

"Yeah, well, that's because you got the good-skin gene in the family," Gretchen complained. "You got Mom's golden skin. You're like the perfect Norwegian goddess."

"Excuse me?" No one had ever called me a goddess before, and I was pretty sure no one would ever do it again, either. Could she at least do it while Sean was still hanging around? And in a very loud voice, with the door wide open? Just shout it: *Kirsten is a goddess!*

"It's not fair. You get to be the cute one," Gretchen complained.

"*Me*? All I ever hear from Mom is about how beautifully you dress and how gorgeous you are and how she wishes I could be put together like you," I said.

"Oh. Really?" Gretchen's mood suddenly perked up a bit.

"Yes," I said.

She laughed at herself. "It's hard to look put together when all you can wear is sweatpants," she said. "One, because your other pants don't fit, and two, because you can't fit anything else over a cast."

"But, ah, you make it look easy," I lied. Then I ran into the kitchen to fetch a mug of coffee for her. "So. What do you have planned for today? Anything?" I asked when I went back to the living room.

"I was thinking maybe we could go shopping—check out the New Year's sales."

Why am I not surprised? I thought. "Sounds good. Hey, Gretch. Does Sean—does he live around here?"

"Two blocks over that way," Gretchen said, pointing. "Isn't he nice?"

"Yeah," I said, snuggling back under the

fleece blanket. *Nice* and *nice-looking*, I thought.

"He's really sweet, not to mention easy on the eyes," Gretchen added. She looked at me as if she were expecting something—for me to completely agree or to start telling her how attracted I was to him.

"He's okay, I guess," I said with a shrug. The last thing I wanted to do was let Gretchen know I was interested in Sean. She'd turn it into a project of hers. Or turn *me* into one, rather. Maybe later, if things worked out . . . but not yet.

Chapter 4

Gretchen and I hit the Ridgedale Mall running—and, in her case, swinging on crutches—in search of clearance items. Well, at least I was hunting for sales. She didn't seem to care about the sales as much as having me drive her to the mall and look after Brett while she shopped.

I was sensing a pattern to my days here that could last for the next month in its entirety.

Fortunately for all of us, the mall had a play area where Brett could run around and scream, and where that was expected rather than frowned upon. He had several partners in crime.

I've never met anyone who likes to shop as much as Gretchen does. She even drives my mom nuts with as much time as she can spend at a mall, which is saying something. My mom and Gretchen were at the Mall of America's grand opening and consider it a pivotal moment in their lives.

We met up in the food court for lunch at noon. Gretchen ordered a Diet Coke while I had a burrito and Brett had a quesadilla, which he insisted on ordering himself, only he pronounced it "cheesy-dill-ah" and I had to translate for him.

Afterward we stopped by a table advertising something called the Polar Bear Plunge when Brett grabbed a keychain off the table before we could stop him. The logo showed a polar bear wearing a scarf, in the middle of doing a dive.

"Sorry," I said as I got Brett to put the keychain back.

"No problem. Have you signed up yet? It's next week, so you still have time to get lots of pledges," the guy manning the table said.

"Pledges?" Gretchen asked.

"It's a fundraiser for the Special Olympics," he explained. "You jump into White Bear Lake, you jump out—you're done."

"And . . . it's next week," I said, the reality of

how cold the water I would be sinking in . . . sinking in.

"Wow. That's a great idea to raise money." Gretchen smiled at him.

I picked up a brochure and skimmed it. I'm not the kind of person who accepts dares just to make a point, but I was almost tempted to sign up. I mean, if it was time for me to start being more outgoing—after all, that was part of my New Year's resolution—I couldn't be more outgoing than to jump into freezing cold water with a bunch of strangers.

"You're considering it, aren't you?" Gretchen said. "You should do it."

"No way. You do it!" I said.

"You're the one who's all, 'this year will be different,' so prove it," she said.

"You're the one who needs the fresh start," I countered.

"Okay, then." Gretchen smiled and turned to the man behind the table. "I have a question. Would you be there to warm us up when we get out of the lake?" she asked him.

I was about to kick her, but then I remembered she already had *one* broken leg.

"Well, I don't know." He smiled at her. "I could be, I guess. Then again, I might need you to warm me up."

"I'll be standing on the shore. So I'll definitely be warm," Gretchen said. "Should I bring you a robe?"

"*Gretchen*," I said, gently pulling her back from the table before she threw herself onto it. "Where's Brett?"

"He's right here," she said. "Clinging to my good leg."

"Oh. Sorry, but I just think . . . you know. Tone it down a little." Maybe I sounded like our mom now, but I didn't care. She was totally embarrassing me!

"What are you talking about?" she replied.

"Should you really flirt with him that much?" I asked.

"Why not?"

"Because. He might . . ."

"Think I like him? What would be the problem there? Honestly, it's like we're from a different gene pool."

But see, that was the point. I'd seen the way she did things and decided I was going to be different. Extremely different.

She knew all about the so-called inner flirt. She had no problem being that way. I, however, felt like a phony whenever I tried it.

I felt badly for pulling her away so abruptly, so I stepped back up to the table.

"Can I make a contribution?" I asked. That wasn't phony, at least. I did want to support Special Olympics, even if I didn't want to do it by jumping into White Bear Lake myself.

"Sure, that would be great." He smiled so nicely at me, I kind of wished he were my age instead of Gretchen's.

Wow, I thought. *I've only been here a few nights and already I'm turning into my sister.*

"Don't forget to check your rearview mirror," Gretchen said, peering over her shoulder as I backed out of the parking spot at the mall.

"Gretchen," I said, trying to keep my composure, "I've been driving for a couple of years. You know that, right?"

"I know, but this is city driving. It's different."

"Yes. Very different. At home, we just back up without looking," I said. "We smash into other people's cars and that's how we figure out when to stop. Every parking lot is a demolition derby, basically."

"Look, Kirsten. It's not funny. It's a well-known fact that teenage drivers are most likely to get into an accident. And if you drive up my insurance rates—"

"I'm still on Mom and Dad's family insurance policy. Don't worry about it," I said.

"Oh. You are?" She sounded a little happier.

"And, I've never had an accident, and I've never even gotten a parking ticket, or speeding ticket, or any kind of ticket. Someone shoved a flyer for a tanning salon under the windshield wiper once, and that's about it."

"Ooh . . . tanning. What a great idea!" Gretchen said, easing back in her seat with a sigh. "You want to go?"

"Not really," I said.

"Of course not. You have, like, the year-round bronze look," Gretchen complained.

"I do not," I said.

"Do too."

I decided not to prolong the argument. I just don't believe in getting the fake bake, myself.

End of story. And it's not because I have anything naturally "golden" about me, except maybe my hair, in the sunlight, in the middle of the summer.

We rode in silence for a few minutes. Then Gretchen said, "Well, do you mind watching Brett while I go?"

"I wanna go tanning!" Brett cried from his seat.

"Little boys don't need tans," Gretchen said to him. "Only mommies need tans. Especially single mommies."

"Aw, come on," Brett complained.

"If you're going to get a tan, Gretchen, you could be ready for the Polar Bear Plunge after all," I said.

"Emphasis on the being a polar bear," she muttered. She frowned at her thighs, but I didn't see what the problem was. I was starting to think she was just obsessing for no reason, because she had nothing else to concentrate on.

"Come on, it's my treat," she urged as we pulled up and parked at the day salon.

"Thanks for the offer, but Brett and I will go to the park so he can play," I said. "I think he'll have more fun there."

"You're such a good mother," she teased.

"Don't even think it. Call my cell when you're done."

"Okay, but don't go too far. I don't want to be sitting here waiting for you forever," she said as I helped her out of the minivan.

So much for gratitude. "Yes, ma'am," I said.

On the way home, we stopped by the local neighborhood grocery store, Zublansky's, for milk, eggs and ice cream for Brett.

I normally don't like grocery stores, but Zublansky's is my definition of heaven. They have everything you could ever think of, and it's all so attractively displayed that it's like going to the Tiffany's of grocery stores. The lighting is even nice.

Gretchen and Brett waited in the car while I ran into the store. I was relieved because things would be so much easier that way. I'd be able to move at a pace faster than a crawl.

I quickly hit the dairy section, and I had to lean halfway into the freezer to pull out a pint of strawberry ice cream from the back of the shelf.

When I emerged, there was a boy standing right behind me, staring at me.

Not just any boy, either. The one who'd returned my lost hat at the lake the other day. The cute one with short auburn hair and green eyes. The one I'd *fallen* on top of.

They were coming out of the woodwork. Or the ice. Or somewhere.

He was wearing an apron with the store's name stitched over the pocket. Unless his name was Zublansky's, Your One-Stop Shop.

"Uh, hi," I said, feeling stupid.

He just looked at me. "Hello."

And then I let the freezer door slam shut on my foot.

Ouch. Don't cry don't cry it doesn't hurt that much, you'll probably only lose two or three toes at most.

"Can I help you find something?" he asked.

"No, no, just fine, just getting some ice cream," I said. I held up the pint and then dropped it into my basket. "Pretty much . . . have it covered," I gasped, with a tiny whimper.

He didn't say anything else. He just walked

away and I stood there, grimacing. Once he was down the aisle, I considered sticking my foot back into the freezer to ice down the swelling. Great, first Gretchen had lost a leg, and now me.

Eventually I limped up to the checkout, where the guy was bagging groceries. I decided to skip his aisle and take the next one over. I had paid and was picking up my bag when he asked, "Need any help out to the car?"

"No thanks. I should be good," I said. "The pain's going away and I just have the one bag, so . . ."

He stared at me. "I wasn't asking you."

I turned to see an elderly woman behind me. "Oh. Right! Well, I can help her," I offered, because there was a long line forming behind me.

"I prefer Conor," she said to me in a snooty voice.

"How are you doing, Mrs. Whitman?" he asked as he went over to pick up her shopping bags.

I couldn't get out to the car fast enough.

Some people you were glad to bump into again. Other people? Not so much.

❋ ❋ ❋

As soon as we got home, I turned on my computer and checked my email. The first thing I saw made my heart sink.

> **FWD: RESERVATION/DEPOSIT
> REQUIRED**
>
> Hey—it's time to send in your
> reservation for Groundhog Getaway!
> We need final totals this week so we
> get a big enough cabin. Fill out and
> print attached form; mail by Friday
> with check or credit card # for
> deposit. Or call the rental agency;
> info attached below.
>
> Thx—Emma

Okay, so it was the day of reckoning—on a small scale, anyway.

Should I go by myself? Should I bluff and sign up for two spaces? Or should I throw in the towel altogether? That would be a *lot* cheaper. I could tell everyone that Gretchen still needed me, that I couldn't *possibly* come.

Of course we were getting a pretty good deal, seeing as how not everyone considered Groundhog Day the perfect weekend for a vacation up North.

I decided to see if Jones was online. She was, so I messaged her right away.

> Hey Jones. Kirst here. Feeling
> especially Cursed.

> I went into the grocery store and who
> do I see but that guy from the skating
> rink, the one who returned my hat,
> and I make a complete idiot out of
> myself, AGAIN.

> My sister just insisted that I clean
> the living room of all my "junk"
> before I even thought about watching
> a movie.

> Why am I here? Again?
> Please remind me because if you
> don't I'm going to run straight home.

Cursed, there is a reason you are there. You are being the good sister. You are doing the world a service. There is another more important reason you are there.

There is? What is it? Besides embarrassing myself in front of guys.

Finding a guy for GG. If I can, you can.

Yes, but you actually have guts. You actually asked someone out before.

So did you. Remember fifth grade?

FIRST grade. We went trick-or-treating together.

So? He said yes, didn't he? This is silly. Get your phone.

My cell started ringing about two seconds later, and when I picked up, the first thing Jones said was that she had bad news. "I was talking to

Keira at school today—"

"What's wrong? How is she?" Keira was another friend of ours. We played on the soccer team together, and our moms had been good friends for a long time.

"Nothing's wrong with her exactly. Well, yes, it is. Something's wrong with her head. She told me she started seeing someone over the holidays. And *then*, you won't believe this, but she told me that it's Tyler. She's dating Tyler," Jones announced.

"That is bad news. For her," I added. "It's good for you, because you were next on his hit-on list—"

"And then she told me that she's already invited him to the cabin," Jones added.

"What?" I gulped. "No way."

"Yeah. Way," Jones replied.

"Why would she . . ."

"I know. It's totally weird. Girl has obviously lost her mind."

I laughed. "No, I didn't mean that—I mean, Tyler's not a totally bad guy. He has his charms."

"Oh, yeah, *sure* he does. I felt like telling her that the cabin was overbooked and she'd have to drop out," Jones said. "I didn't. Of course. She was in on this from the beginning, so it's not like we can un-invite her."

"Great." I tried to smile as Jones told me some funny stories about her own attempts to find a guy for Groundhog Getaway, but as we said goodbye and I clicked off my phone, I felt this tightness in my chest. Now that Keira was seeing Tyler, I was *really* under pressure to find a date for the weekend.

I picked up my phone again and dialed the number for the cabin rental company. When a woman answered, I gave her Emma's last name, and told her I would need space. For two people.

Sean's image immediately came to mind. I could so easily see the two of us hanging out, having a good time. And I could see Tyler looking at us and having a huge pang of regret because that could have been him with me. Sean and I would skate together, we'd hold hands, we'd snuggle by the cabin fire . . .

"You're all set," the woman on the phone said.

"Great." I tapped my credit card against the desk and stared out the bedroom window. Now which house exactly was Sean's?

Chapter 5

$\mathcal{E}$arly the next morning, I was in the kitchen emptying the dishwasher when the doorbell rang.

I started to dash for the front door, hoping it might be Sean. I didn't know why I thought he'd be dropping by, but that didn't matter—I was either hoping, or praying, that it might be him. I didn't stop to be rational.

But then I paused and checked my reflection in the hallway mirror before I answered the door, the way Gretchen told me that I should. When I finally took a deep breath and opened the door, I saw a FedEx truck parked out front, and a woman in uniform disappearing down the front walk. "Thanks!" I called to her as I spotted the box she'd left on our doorstep.

She turned around and gave me a small wave as she climbed into the driver's seat.

So much for worrying about being put together nicely with my hair brushed.

The package was addressed to both me and Gretchen, and it was from Mom. There were about a dozen "Fragile" and "Perishable" stickers on the box. When I opened it, I wasn't surprised to see a big rectangular Tupperware container full of cupcakes. Mom's number-one choice for care packages. She'd sent them to me at summer camp at least twice.

"She didn't," Gretchen said, as soon as she saw me standing in the doorway with the box in my hand. "Mom knows I'm trying to lose weight. She can be such a sabotager when she wants to be!"

"I think the word you're looking for is *saboteur*," I said.

"Actually, I think the *words* I'm looking for are *no cupcakes*." She glared at me. "Get them out of here."

"Trashcan okay?" I pointed to the kitchen garbage can, wondering how many I could take out of the box and eat or save for later. I at least wanted to have *one*.

"No. That's not good enough."

"You're in a lovely mood."

I heard a scream coming from upstairs, so I left the cupcakes on the counter and quickly ran up to check on Brett, since Gretchen couldn't easily do it.

Luckily, nothing was wrong. He was just practicing his superhero role: Caped Screamer Boy. He was jumping from his bed to the floor with a pillowcase on his shoulders. Over and over again.

"Come on, buddy. You should be downstairs," I said. "Grandma sent cupcakes!"

"Cupcakes!" Brett screamed, and he ran for the stairs. I grabbed his hands to help him "fly" down the stairs (if I hadn't, he'd have flown right to the bottom with a concussion).

When we ran into the kitchen, the container of cupcakes had vanished, and the garbage disposal was running loudly as Gretchen stood over the sink, her hand on the faucet.

Watching Gretchen annihilate those cupcakes was like a scene out of a horror movie. There ought to have been loud, screechy music playing, except that you wouldn't be able to hear it over the sound of frosting and cake being ground to bits.

"Could we have at least saved a couple for Brett?" I asked as she finally switched off the disposal and she could hear me. "And me?"

"Sorry," she said. She looked at Brett. "The cupcakes got spoiled in the mail—sorry, honey. How about a yogurt?" As she pulled one out of the fridge for Brett, she whispered to me, "I cannot have cake around."

"So for Brett's birthday party at the end of the month, what are you going to have? Carrot sticks?" I asked.

She handed Brett a spoon for his yogurt, and he dashed into the TV room to watch PBS.

"No, of course not. Don't be ridiculous. I'll serve celery." She laughed. "No, actually, I'll order a cake from the bakery. And I won't eat any of it. Come on, just help me a little, okay? You know how much I love Mom's cupcakes. The woman can't cook a roast to save her life, but she can bake. These things are lethal. There are about a thousand calories in each one."

"You're crazy, you know that?" I said. "Mom

sent those specially for us. What are we going to tell her? Thanks, your cupcakes grind up really easily? I think you overreacted."

"Maybe slightly," she agreed as she dried her hands on a dishtowel. "But I already had ice cream yesterday when I shouldn't have, and I have to get back on course. I just have to."

"No, you know what you need, Gretch?" I said. "You need to get out of the house more. Make some new friends."

"You're talking to someone with a broken leg, and it's the middle of winter," she replied in an irritated tone.

"So?" I shrugged. "Mind over matter."

She glared at me as if maybe she was about to put me through the garbage disposal as well.

"Okay, I'm sorry. You're in a bad way. I just want to help, okay? I was thinking we could just make a couple of routines, like, we go out for coffee every day. That way we'll meet people."

"I *know* people," she said. "It's just that—well, a lot them were both our friends. Mine and Luke's. So it's awkward. And I know I need a new routine, and a job, and new friends, but it's so hard to get around with my leg like this!" I'd never heard Gretchen sound so frustrated.

"So, we'll drive," I said. "You'll have to go like ten steps, at most."

"True. But do we want to take Brett to a coffee shop?"

"Sure. Why not?"

"Because then it wouldn't be as much fun for us, we couldn't just relax. We'd have to keep track of him. He'd spill coffee, he'd bug people. He'd bug us."

Sometimes I really wondered why Gretchen had wanted to have a child so much. It was like she couldn't handle the responsibility, or at least, she didn't want to. Then again, I had no experience being a mostly-single parent, so what did I know? "What are we going to do . . . leave him here?" I asked.

"No! I was just thinking . . . maybe while he's watching *Shrek* for the eighty-ninth time, you could go to the bakery down the street and bring some coffee back for me and a treat for Brett. And maybe take Bear for a walk while you're at it. Please?"

This life as Super Nanny was really shaping up nicely. I got to take the dog for a walk when it was ten degrees outside. Lucky me! "But Gretch. You won't meet anyone that way."

"I know, and you have a point. But give me until next week, okay? With all this snow . . . it's just too hard to get around without wiping out. I'm completely exhausted from yesterday."

"I don't know," I said.

"*And*, you pass Sean's house on the way to the bakery," she said.

"Oh. Really? Okay. I'll go," I said with a smile. Though I was dreading the cold, I was actually dying for a chance to get out of the house by myself for a little while. And the way Bear was racing around the house, chasing Brett and his tail simultaneously, made me realize he needed the exercise, too. "But do I need to come right back, or can I hang out there a little while and write?"

"Stay as long as you want to," she said as she jotted down the directions for me.

The bakery was only about an eight-block walk from Gretchen's house. I went really slowly at first, just in case Sean was home, just in case he wanted to come running out and join me for coffee.

But of course, he had a life. I was the one wandering aimlessly.

As I walked up the block toward the bakery, the wonderful scents of bread and sweet things baking got stronger and stronger. I was definitely about to get pulled into the pastry vortex.

Actually, the way Bear pulled on the leash, I was about to get pulled all over Minneapolis. He could use another puppy obedience course—or two. Not that I knew how to train him. I'd never had a dog before. Gretchen had decided to get Bear for a couple of reasons—one, to entertain Brett, and two, to make her feel more safe about living on her own. I didn't know how Bear would do that, except attack a burglar by licking his face.

Anyway, in typical Gretchen fashion, she'd gone for the dog that looked the cutest when she went to the humane society to adopt a puppy. And Bear had been cute, when he was three months old, before he turned into a gigantic white furry beast.

I tied Bear to the *Star Tribune* newspaper box while I went inside the bakery. When I leaned over to wrap the leash around the pole, Bear gave me a huge smack on the lips. "Mmm. Thanks, Bear." Now I couldn't say I'd never been kissed in the Twin Cities.

I walked into the bakery and just stood by the front door for a second, looking around at the tables and booths, and inhaling the delicious aromas. Then I noticed a guy behind the counter watching me, from where he was leaning against the bakery case, a paperback book propped in his hands.

"Hi," I said, walking over to him. "Wow. Everything looks so *good*." *Oh God*, I thought. *Did I just look at a guy and tell him everything looked so* good?

Hold on. As I walked closer I realized he was the Zublansky's dairy aisle guy, and the one I'd nearly knocked down at the skating rink, and the one who brought me my hat.

"Can I get you something?" he asked, glancing up from his book. He didn't seem to recognize me — or if he did, he didn't want to acknowledge me.

I quickly looked down to hide my embarrassment and checked out all of the rolls, croissants, and donuts. "I'll take a cinnamon roll. And a double latte, please."

"Sure thing." He set down his book and grabbed a plate and a small piece of paper wrap to pick up the roll. "You look kind of familiar," he said.

"I saw you at the lake. The skating rink. New Year's Eve day?" I said.

"Why did you say it like a question? Weren't you there?"

"Of course I was. I mean, I think I'd know if I weren't there," I said. "I mean, I'd have to not be . . . there." Oh, god, I sounded like an idiot.

"Ah. How true." He didn't mention the other time we'd seen each other, when I tried to carry out groceries for another customer at Zublansky's. For that I'd be eternally grateful. Or at least grateful for the next ten minutes.

"Did you just move into the neighborhood?" he asked.

I shook my head. "No, I don't live here. I'm just staying with my sister for a while."

"Oh."

"For a month."

"Oh."

I had to be more interesting. It was time to bring out the inner flirt. Even if it didn't work with him, at least this would count as practice.

"I've never been here before," I said. "To this bakery. It's really nice."

He looked up over the espresso machine at me, with a perfectly blank expression.

"So you've never been here before?" A woman who'd been slicing loaves of bread turned to me with a smile. She looked like she was in her twenties. She had short, black hair and wore lots of silver jewelry, including three ear piercings and a nose ring. "It can't be the incredibly helpful clerks, can it? Conor, your reputation precedes you."

Conor, that's a nice name, I thought. I'd never known anyone named Conor before.

"We used to go to this other bakery, but my sister got into an argument with the owner because her wedding cake wasn't perfect." I rolled my eyes. "My sister can be a piece of work."

"Mine too," the woman agreed.

"I mean, actually the cake was very nice, and I think it was everything it was supposed to be. But she said something about how the little figurines on top were supposed to be personalized, so they looked like her, and the figurine was too big or something . . ."

I'm babbling, I thought. *I'm completely making a fool of myself.*

"My sister is a control freak with a bad self image," I explained, and the girl gave me a sympathetic nod.

"Got one of those at home, too," she said.

"Double latte," Conor said in a flat voice as he set a giant mug on the counter. "And we don't do wedding cakes. In case you were wondering."

"No. I wasn't. No need for wedding cakes here," I said. Not now. Probably not ever, at this rate.

"Don't let him get to you," Conor's co-worker said to me. "This is what happens when you give a night person a morning person's job."

"Hey, Paula, you're not exactly Mary Sunshine yourself," he replied with a frown.

"Thank God," she said. "Hi. I'm Paula."

"Kirsten," I said. "Nice to meet you."

"So. What are you doing here?" Conor said to me. "Shouldn't you be in school or something?"

This guy gave the phrase "Minnesota Nice" a whole new meaning. Or took it all away, rather. "Likewise?" I said.

"Oh, he's done with school. He's Mr. AP Class." Paula bagged a loaf of bread and fastened a twist tie to close it.

"I am not."

"He has nothing else to do but hang out here and insult customers." She poked his arm with a wooden stir stick and then tapped his ear with it.

"And co-workers. Don't forget co-workers." He swatted at the stir stick as if it were a fly. "I'm taking some time off before I start college in the fall. Well, actually, first I'm saving money to go backpacking through Europe this summer."

"Slacker," Paula muttered.

"I'm going to Europe, too," I said. "Well, England. Then maybe Europe."

He covered his mouth as he yawned.

"Well, talk to you later. Maybe when you wake up," I said, and Paula laughed.

So much for flirting practice.

I went over to a table near the window, pulled up a chair, and opened my backpack. I wish I had one of those cool, really thin computers, but of course I don't, because my parents are saving money to send me to college next year and I don't make enough to buy my own. So I have the one my dad bought for himself about three years ago. It's had more upgrades than Janice Dickinson on "America's Next Top Model" (one of my favorite indulgent wastes of time) has had plastic surgery.

Anyway, it might not have been the newest, but at least it had a wireless card, so I could surf and email while I sat there trying to work on my Independent Study.

I looked up a few times as I head Conor joking around with other customers. He was funny and light-hearted with them . . . so why not with me? Why'd he have to give me such a hard time? Maybe he still resented me for nearly knocking him to the ice. That could sway a person's opinion, I guess.

I felt like I should get to know him a little better. After all, it couldn't hurt to try to meet as many guys as possible while I was here—or at least more than one. The old "putting all your eggs in one basket" theory. Although I didn't really want to think about my eggs.

"So how long are you in town?" Paula asked when I went up for a refill.

"A month or so. I'm basically finished with school already, so they let me spend some time away working on my Independent Study."

"Which is?" Conor asked, again in that blasé tone of his.

"It's a collection of all kinds of writing. Stories, poems, letters, emails, IMs—"

"Since when are IMs worth collecting?" he scoffed.

"Oh. Well, maybe yours aren't," I said with a shrug.

Paula started laughing, while Conor looked at me as if I were the rudest person on Earth. Which I guess I sort of sounded like, but come on—he'd been equally insulting to me.

"So what are you saying? They're letting you turn in a *scrapbook* as your final project?

What kind of school is this?" Conor asked.

I felt like punching him. "It's not a scrap-book," I said. "And it's a very good school. Very."

I went back to my seat, and after sifting through some writing of mine, looking for poetry to include in my project, I couldn't resist emailing.

> Jones, remember skating/hat/grocery
> checkout boy? I think he's following
> me—his name is Conor and

"That one going to make it into the book?"

Conor was wiping down the table next to me, which a couple of other customers had just vacated, leaving plates and mugs behind.

"Uh—I'm sorry?" I quickly hit the minimize button and made my silly IM disappear.

He must have seen me hit the delete key, because he said, "I thought you were writing things worth collecting."

"Well, no. I mean, some things are worth saving, and some aren't. And see, that's the point of the project, to determine, like, what you save . . . and what you get rid of. And what that means." As I was talking, I felt my face turning bright red. He was staring at me with his eyebrows slightly raised, as if I'd had too much coffee and was just ranting and raving.

Which I was.

"So that wasn't worth keeping. Does the person you wrote to know that? Or share the same opinion?"

"No, of course not. She thinks it's brilliant, like everything I write."

"She must be a really good friend, then."

I narrowed my eyes and glared at him.

Then all of a sudden there was this strange grating noise coming from the street. It sounded like someone was pushing a shovel against the cement and pulling it back and forth. It was like nails on a chalkboard, only ten thousand times worse.

"I think that dog's had enough," Conor commented as he gazed out the window and up the block. "Who would be dumb enough to tie their dog to a newspaper rack in the middle of winter? Talk about cruel."

Bear! I realized. *Oh no!*

Conor went back into the kitchen. Thank

God he was gone—didn't he already think I was awful?

I jammed my computer into my backpack without even turning it off, left my mug on the table and just grabbed my jacket and ran out the door. I felt terrible. I'd completely forgotten about Bear. I wasn't used to having a dog! He was attempting to drag the newspaper box down the street. He had gotten one side of it unbolted somehow, and he was turning it and running around in circles.

"Oh no, Bear—I'm sorry!" I said as I ran over to him.

He jumped on me to lick my face. It wasn't long before he had the leash wrapped around my legs, and I was about to go down with the *Star Tribune* box.

Please don't be looking out the window, I thought as I slowly and carefully untangled the leash. I unclipped Bear's collar for a second, and miraculously, he didn't run off. He just sat there waiting for me while I unhooked the leash from the newspaper box and then tried to reset the box so that it didn't look like it had just been vandalized.

Then I realized Bear wasn't being obedient and sitting there waiting for me. He was waiting for Sean, who was walking toward us. Of all the luck. Did I have time to grab a piece of gum? Fix my hair? Anything?

Big city, but small neighborhood, I guess. I'd always heard that about cities, but I didn't know how true it was.

"Hey! Kirsten, right?" he said.

I nodded. "Hi. How's it going?"

"This puppy's got some serious energy, doesn't he?" He leaned down to scratch Bear behind the ears.

"The problem is that he doesn't realize he's not a puppy anymore." I smiled. "I think I'm going to have to start taking him for really long walks. Or run a marathon or something."

"You run marathons?" Sean asked, looking impressed—or startled, I wasn't sure.

"Oh, yeah. Sure. Doesn't everyone?" I laughed nervously. "I mean, when I have to, I will. Like if I were being chased, I'm sure I could move quickly." I was babbling like a fool. I was saying nothing that made sense. Why did I insist on making the *least* out of this situation?

"You plan on being chased?" Sean asked.

Well, it would be nice, I thought as I looked into his eyes. "Not exactly," I said.

"Good. Hey, you should come down to the lake tomorrow. You know, like we talked about?"

"Oh. Yeah?" I asked. Did I ever say anything else when he was around? I got so tongue-tied, it was ridiculous. "I mean, yes, I should. Shouldn't I? It would be fun."

There was an awkward pause.

Come on, I urged myself. If you don't make something happen right now, you might never be lucky enough to see this guy again. Who knows if it'll snow again while you're here? You can't rely on Mother Nature to get you on a date.

"So when do you work at the rink?" I asked.

"I'll be there tomorrow morning," he said. "Nine until noon. Is tomorrow good for you?"

It is now, I thought. *It's a whole lot better, in fact.* "We'll try to make it," I said, not wanting to sound too anxious about it. Just keep things casual—until I could tackle him.

And then Bear saw a squirrel and dragged me away before I could say anything else, which was probably a good thing.

Chapter 6

The first thing I saw when I woke up the next morning was frost on the window. I snuggled under the down comforter, where I was cozy and warm. I didn't see a reason to jump out of bed.

And then I remembered: Sean had said he'd be at the rink that morning. We had a semi-date set up. I had to get down there!

I threw back the comforter, swung my legs over the edge of the bed, stood up, and found my slippers and my fleece sweatshirt as quickly as I could. The house was so cold in the morning that you had to be prepared. Besides, you never knew when you were going to end up in the driveway in your pajamas. Ahem.

I went downstairs, opened the door and

grabbed the morning newspaper from the top step. I shook it open to the weather section, where it said today would be a high of ten degrees. Not the best weather to take a toddler skating. But Brett was tough. Besides, I'd put so many layers on him that he'd be unable to move, but he'd be warm enough.

When I told Gretchen that we were going down to the lake, she looked up from reading the morning newspaper. "The UV Index today is zero point three. That's the risk of getting a sunburn or skin damage. Why do they even bother reporting that? Anything under five is completely useless. Anyway, I don't know about the skating. I thought you could spend the morning cleaning."

"Uh . . . I could?" *Quick. Think of something,* I told myself.

"Well, unless you have another idea," Gretchen said.

If I told her I was going down there to see Sean, she might even be supportive. But I didn't want her knowing that I liked him, for some reason. She'd only tease me and tell me I didn't have the right outfit on or something.

"Actually, the thing is, Gretch, I've signed Brett up for skating lessons. Well, hockey lessons. And the class starts this morning." I looked up at the clock. "At ten." That should give me enough time to get Brett ready to go, and to make myself look decent in however many layers it would take for me not to get frostbite. Also, I didn't want to seem too eager by showing up at 9:01.

We didn't actually have to skate long. We just had to see Sean and I had to talk to him and make him fall in love with me, or at least crush on me enough to go away with me for a weekend. That could happen in the warm rec building as well as on the ice. In fact I'd prefer going inside. It could take him a few minutes to get from barely knowing me to loving me.

"Really? Hockey lessons?" Gretchen didn't sound as if she believed me. "For Brett? But he's only three. He doesn't even skate all that well yet. How's he going to handle a hockey stick?"

"Oh, that won't be a problem. See, it's a class just for little kids like him," I explained. "The rec center offers them. I signed him up when we were there the other day."

"I didn't see anything about classes there."

"Yes, but you didn't come inside," I reminded her. This was turning out to be the longest, most complicated lie in history. Why couldn't she just be glad we were getting out of her hair for a while? "It was posted on the bulletin board outside the office."

She just stared at me.

"Big neon green sheet. You really didn't see it?"

Still she was giving me that look of disbelief. Why would I make up children's hockey lessons?

"Well, the class starts today. I'd better get Brett ready to go." If I acted like it was true, then it would be true.

"Aunt Kirsten, we can't skate here. We can't!" Brett kept saying over and over as we stepped into the rink.

"Sure we can," I said. I was holding Brett's hands and guiding him along.

In the other rink on the lake, a bunch of guys were playing hockey. Choosing the empty rink seemed like a wise move to me. Considering I'd stumbled down the ramp on our way to the rink, nearly stepping on Brett with my skate, things were fine now. Things were perfect in fact. Sean was playing hockey, and when he was done, we'd talk, and—

"Aunt Kirsten we can't," Brett said again. "Mommy said—"

"Look, I realize I'm not the best skater, but this will be fine," I insisted.

Suddenly a guy skated up behind us. Well, he wasn't skating exactly—he was sliding on sneakers. "What the heck do you think you're doing?" he asked in a gruff tone.

"I'm sorry?" I said.

"This is a broomball rink," he said. "Didn't you see the sign?"

And as soon as I glanced at the side of the rink, I noticed a sign on the wooden boards: BROOMBALL ONLY. NO SKATING. Actually there were about six signs like that, I saw as I scanned the rink. I'd been so busy checking out Sean that I hadn't noticed.

"I'm really sorry—I'm just visiting," I said as I helped Brett off the ice. "I didn't know."

"Well, now you do. Sneakers only, okay? Get out," he practically barked.

"Aunt Kirsten, Mommy always says we can't skate here," Brett repeated. "I told you."

"I know, sweetie. I'm sorry." I gave him a little hug. Next time I would listen to Brett more carefully. "Sorry, again," I said as we gently glided out of the rink.

"*Read* next time," the guy said in an angry voice.

"Sue us next time," I muttered under my breath.

Fortunately, the game broke up a minute later and Sean skated over to us. "Ignore that guy, he's insane."

"Really."

"Really. We've been trying to tell him that for years. I mean, you shouldn't be on that rink wearing skates, but it's not the end of the world. It's not like you barged in during a game."

"It seems like I have this habit of getting yelled at by the rink police," I said.

"Rink police? Is that what you call us?" he asked.

"I don't know," I said. "Isn't that the right term?"

"Not exactly. But don't worry. You didn't even make it around the rink once, so I don't think you did that much damage." He rested his chin on his hockey stick and smiled at me. "We'll go easy on you this time."

How could I resist someone who looked at me like that? He was absolutely, extremely handsome. "Thanks. So. Anything going on here? Like a broomball game?" I asked.

"Nah. You just missed a pickup hockey game with some friends. Nothing special. Although my brother made a great save."

"Save?"

"He's a goalie. Goalies are strange. Did you know that? They're obsessed."

"And . . . this is your brother you're talking about?" I asked.

"Yeah. And he's even crazier than most goalies. Which means he's *way* over the top." Sean laughed. "He already took off for work, but you'll meet him sometime, and then you'll see what I mean."

Ooh! This sounded promising. He was actually talking about me meeting his brother. That implied meeting the rest of his family. His parents.

Wait, I wasn't ready for that. *We'd* barely just met.

Quit getting carried away, I told myself. So far you're just friends, or vague acquaintances. Flirt. Think of a way to flirt. Do what Crystal or Emma would do.

It was hard to think of a way to look sexy or attractive when I knew my nose was red from the cold, my face was almost completely covered by a striped scarf, and if my lips weren't chapped it was a miracle.

While Sean skated around with Brett for a minute, I quickly fished my strawberry lip balm out of my pocket and ran it across my lips a few dozen times, hoping at least a tiny bit would sink in and last for the next ten minutes.

While I was doing that, my cell phone started to ring. I fumbled for it in my jacket pocket, then nearly dropped it because I was wearing my mittens. "Hey, Emma," I said as I finally answered it. "It's really strange you called right now because I was just thinking of you."

"You were?" Emma asked.

"You must have sensed it," I told her.

"Actually, what I sensed was that I have no idea what to do here. See, I really wanted to invite Cameron to the cabin. So I was about to, you know, but then Mike called and he's like, can we get back together because I really, really missed you over Christmas." Emma went on for a few more minutes, describing the complicated situation.

"So, what are you going to do?" I asked.

"That's the thing. I really don't know. I mean, obviously I still have feelings for Mike, but then Cameron's so sweet, and he gave me that bracelet for Christmas, and I know he *thinks* I'm going to invite him because I've been talking about it."

I would kill to have those kinds of problems. Instead, there I was, chilled to the bone, trying to initiate at least one conversation with a guy who I barely knew. Which reminded me—I'd better get back to work.

"Emma—I can't really talk right now," I said as Sean skated back toward me. "Can I call you later?"

"Okay," she said with a sigh. "But I really don't know what to do."

"You'll figure it out," I told her. "Don't worry!" I clicked off my phone. "That was my friend Emma," I explained to Sean. "Her nickname is Emma Dilemma because everything's a big crisis for her."

I wanted to say: Speaking of a crisis . . . we're planning this weekend. It's in about a month. I've committed to bringing a date. Emma has two possible dates, while I seem to have none. Wouldn't you love to come with me?

"So, are there, ah, lessons or classes or something?" I asked instead.

Sean smiled. "In broomball?"

"Sure. That, or skating in general."

"I don't know. I mean, sure, probably—for kids. That's what you mean, right? For Brett here?"

"Uh . . . sure." I smiled. "For Brett."

We both knew they were for me, but he was nice enough not to tease me.

"I could, you know. Show him a few things."

"Really?" My voice squeaked as I said that, and I cringed at the sound of my inner flirt. She needed practice. Badly.

"Should I get him?" I asked, in a more normal tone. I looked around and saw Brett sitting on the side of the lake, on a snow bank, molding shapes with the snow. He seemed safe there, but I'd have to keep a close eye on him. That boy could get into trouble in seconds, even if he would be slowed down by his skates.

Fortunately Gretchen had insisted on making him wear a bicycle helmet, so at least I didn't have to worry about him cracking his head open on the ice.

"Well, maybe it would be easier if I showed you first," Sean said.

"Oh. Oh?" I said.

Man, did I need to work on this talking-to-boys thing. I sounded like an idiot.

Sean took off his hockey gloves and got rid of his stick and helmet. "What do you want to know?" he asked.

"Well . . . the most important thing I can't do is stop," I said.

"Yeah. I noticed that." He grinned as he came over and put his hands on my waist. Just like the last time when he'd done this, I could feel his hands were warm. "Watch my skates," Sean said. "Ready?" He stopped so suddenly that he had to grab me and keep me from falling over. "You have to push against the outer edge of your skate blade. Let it catch the ice."

"Okay. I hear what you're saying, but I still don't get it," I said.

We skated back and forth in front of Brett, so I could keep an eye on him. Sean patiently showed me how to turn on my skates, and what angle I needed to use in order to push the blade away from me and have it catch the ice and therefore stop. It was sort of like skiing, but more scary because we were on the ice. I had this urge to tell Sean that he could *show* me how to stop, but that I wasn't *going* to stop.

"Watch me again," he said, and he skated in what must have been slow motion for him, to demonstrate how it was done. "Okay, your turn," he said.

I couldn't wait until we were done and I could call Emma back and tell her about this private lesson. She would die. If I didn't die first.

Wait a second, I thought as I tried to push off with my skate. Speaking of dying. I couldn't feel my feet anymore. "Maybe I—maybe I should get going," I said.

"Really?" Sean looked disappointed, which I took as a good sign.

"Yeah." I nodded.

"Come on, stay," he urged. "You're starting to get it! Plus, this is fun."

"The thing is . . . my feet. I actually can't feel my toes exactly." Somehow I hadn't noticed this fact in all the time I'd been there, but it was suddenly very true, and very painful. I hadn't felt cold, but now my extremities seemed like they were about to fall off.

"I'll get Brett, you go inside," Sean said. "Now. Hurry up."

I nodded and sort of staggered up the wooden ramp to the building. Inside, the heater was blowing at full blast and I sat on a bench, shivering.

Sean and Brett came in and Sean crouched down in front of both of us. "You guys gonna be okay?" He started to unlace my skates, then Brett's. "I'm off in like ten minutes. Can you wait for me? Then I can drive you guys home."

"You can . . . come for lunch," I said between chattering teeth.

"Sounds good. Put your feet right there." He pointed to a heating vent in the floor. "Don't move them until I get back."

"So, how were the hockey lessons?" Gretchen asked when we walked into the house. She was sitting on the sofa with her laptop computer.

"The what?" Sean replied.

I coughed and then cleared my throat. It wasn't such a big lie I'd told, but I definitely didn't want Gretchen to start harping on me about how I had to be more honest with her. "Brett's hockey class," I said. "See, I thought there was a class. But I guess I read the sheet wrong."

"Yeah, we have a league, for kids of all ages, but no official classes," Sean told her.

"We learned some things anyway," I said. "Didn't we, Brett?" Like how nice it is to skate with Sean and how he's the perfect height for me.

"Until we got a little on the frozen side. Then it wasn't so fun."

"Kirsten, you never wear enough clothes," Gretchen said.

"Oh, really?" Sean smiled at me, as if that weren't necessarily a bad characteristic to have. "Actually, I did notice that when she ran outside in her pajamas the other morning."

"And then she wonders why she's never warm enough," Gretchen said. "What do you think? Maybe she's cold-blooded. Does that mean she's cold-hearted, too?"

"Oh, yeah. In fact not only am I cold and unfeeling, I'm a reptile, basically. Thanks, Gretch."

"Well, you did fall through the ice when you were two," she reminded me—not that I had any memory of the event, just of this story being told every year at about the time everyone was asking, "Is the lake frozen yet?" I was like the poster child for waiting for a deep freeze before venturing onto questionable ice.

"Think about it," Gretchen said. "Maybe that has something to do with the fact you can't keep warm, Kirst."

Or, maybe it's the fact that I am Cursed, I thought.

"You did?" Sean asked. "Let me guess. Were you trying to learn how to skate?"

I glared at him, but I couldn't help smiling when I saw the look he was giving me. Half amused and half flirty. "It was the pond near our house. I think Gretchen was the one who thought it'd be a nice idea to teach me how to skate even though the ice wasn't thick enough yet."

"Oh, no, you're not blaming this on me," Gretchen said with a laugh. "You ran out onto the ice. No one could stop you. Then we heard this awful cracking noise."

"Sounds like something Brett would do," Sean commented.

"Doesn't it, though?" I agreed. "We must share the same genetic adventure . . . ous . . . ness."

We both looked at each other and grinned. He seemed interested. Was he, though, or was he just being friendly?

There was no way I'd find out with Gretchen and Brett around. It was hard to really talk with

Gretchen sitting right there. Couldn't she tell we needed some alone time?

But no. She refused to move off the living room couch from the hours of 9 A.M. to 9 P.M., making privacy a little difficult. She was starting to learn all the TV schedules. She knew soap opera plotlines. She'd seen all the TLC makeover shows at least twice.

"I wonder if we could go somewhere maybe like . . . without Brett sometime," I said. I looked meaningfully at Gretchen. She didn't respond.

"You know what would be fun? Before school starts again and I get totally busy, a bunch of us could go skiing at Buck Hill or something," Sean said.

"That sounds perfect—"

"No way," Gretchen interrupted me.

"Yes way," I said, looking at Sean. Did she seriously think I couldn't have *one* afternoon off to go out with Sean?

"I'm telling you, Kirst, don't go skiing. You'll break something."

"No, I won't. What do you think, because you broke your leg skiing at Lutsen, I'm going to break mine?" I asked.

"And if you break your leg, too, we're going to be in such deep trouble—" she went on, not even listening to me.

"I wouldn't!" I cried.

"Kirsten. You're not the best skier. Be honest."

I couldn't believe her. Why was she trying to shoot me down in front of Sean all the time? She thought it was funny, but it wasn't. "What? There's nothing wrong with my skiing."

"Remember the time you wiped out going down Lutsen Mountain and you nearly impaled yourself on a rock, and Mom and Dad had a heart attack?"

I glared at her. Did she have to tell every embarrassing story in the world about me to Sean? "Gretch? I was seven. It was the bunny run."

"Still." Gretchen started laughing. "Your legs wrapped around you three times. You looked like a pretzel. See, Kirsten was super tall and skinny for her age. Her legs practically went up to here." She tapped her shoulders.

Sean looked at me and smiled, and I sort of sank down on the sofa, trying to look shorter. I am *not* all out of proportion, I wanted to say.

My body has all the necessary parts now. I went through some major growth spurts, okay?

He was looking at me with a kind of knowing smile. "You still have long legs," he said.

"Come on, Sean. Let's go to the kitchen and make lunch," I said. "You're probably hungry and I know I am. And so is Brett."

"I'll have a salad!" Gretchen called to us before she turned the volume back up on the TV.

"Which you can make yourself," I muttered. "The great thing about my big sister is how incredibly *supportive* she can be," I said as I got some bread, cheese, turkey and other fixings out of the fridge.

"What do you mean?" Sean asked.

I shook my head. "She just—like, she still has to get her shots in. Like we're still kids or something." But that didn't make sense, since we'd never really been kids at the same time, had we? Not exactly, anyway. Was she making up for lost time, since she couldn't exactly pick fights with me when she was eight and I was two?

"Okay, so if she's dead set against me skiing, that doesn't mean we can't do something else,"

I said. "How about tomorrow? I mean, I was going to ask if you were, you know, free."

"In the afternoon I am," he said.

"Okay, so how about like, ah . . ."

"How about something indoors?" Sean said. "Since we don't want your frostbite to kick in again."

"That would be bad, wouldn't it?" I smiled, thinking that I liked the sound of "indoors." Was I supposed to suggest snuggling on the sofa at his house and watching a movie? There was a fine line between being a flirt and sounding desperate. I'd never had a chance to cross the line, myself, but I'd seen others sprint past it.

"Well, not to do the typical out-of-town visitor thing, but have you been to the Mall of America yet?" Sean asked.

I nodded. "Sure, a few times, but I can always go again. That sounds fun." I'd have to make sure I didn't mention it to Gretchen, or she'd insist on coming along. She couldn't resist the pull of the mall.

"We could walk around, maybe go to a movie. I have hockey practice all morning and a game at night. How about three o'clock or something like that?"

"Perfect," I said. "I'll just clear it with Gretchen and then—"

"Clear it?" he asked. "What, is she like in charge of you?"

"No! No, of course not," I said. "It's just that I'm sort of in charge of taking care of Brett. Since she can't move around as quickly as Brett does."

"No one can," Sean joked. "He can be out the door and across the street before you even blink."

"Exactly!" I said. "He's very fast. So I'll just make sure she knows she has to be here— set him up with a video or whatever."

"Sounds good," he said, settling into a stool at the kitchen counter. "So what kind of sandwiches are you making?"

I grinned. "Grilled. Hot. Something like that. You like cheese? Turkey and cheese?"

"Make three for me, okay?" Sean turned on the TV in the kitchen and quickly found a college basketball game to watch. I handed him a bag of potato chips that I'd stashed in an out-of-the-way cabinet so that they didn't tempt Gretchen.

After I put four sandwiches together and put them onto the panini grill, I quickly threw a small salad together for Gretchen. I carried the bottle of low-everything dressing in for her, with a PB&J sandwich for Brett.

"Did you ask him to look after me when I was here, or something?" I asked her in a low voice as I set the food on the coffee table in front of her.

"No. What are you talking about?"

"Nothing. Never mind," I said. I just wanted to make sure that whatever was happening . . . was happening because it could. Not because it should. "Enjoy your lunch!"

When I went back into the kitchen, Sean was polishing off the bag of chips. I grabbed a couple of sodas from the fridge and handed him one. Somehow I had a feeling that my lunch would be a lot more fun than Gretchen's.

Chapter 7

$\mathcal{M}ore$ snow, I thought as I was standing by the front door, looking out at Sean at the end of the driveway. Already this winter it had snowed more than last year, and it was still early January. Should I write a thank-you letter to Mother Nature? Or to the KARE-11 meteorologist who had forecast it the night before, giving me fair warning to get up early and be dressed this time?

Gretchen came up behind me as I was standing there, and nearly scared me to death. "Why don't you see if he wants a hot chocolate?" she asked.

I nearly jumped. I had been so absorbed in thinking about Sean and what to do that I hadn't even noticed her or heard her footsteps—

or crutch steps. "What?"

"Well, it's cold out there. I had to farm out the shoveling. But now that you're here, I guess I can cancel it — I hadn't even thought of that."

"No!" I nearly cried. "Don't *fire* him. I mean, uh, my arms — they're not that strong. And what if we get one of those blizzards where it takes the entire morning to clear the drive —"

"You've really turned into a worrywart since I left home," Gretchen interrupted my raving.

"What? Me? No," I said.

"Well, then, if I didn't know better, I could swear you have a crush."

"No, I don't," I protested. "Still, out of the kindness of my heart, I will go make him a hot chocolate, I think."

I put the teakettle on the stove to boil, and then I went upstairs and brushed my hair again, and pulled my favorite hat over it, positioning it just so. I stopped in the bathroom to brush a little blush onto my cheeks. Then, back downstairs in the kitchen, I stirred the hot chocolate in a plastic, commuter mug, tossed in some mini marshmallows, and snapped on the lid.

I took a deep breath, summoned my inner flirt, and went outside. I decided to sneak up on Sean. I'd decided the night before that it was time for me to make my move—if this was the New Year, New Kirsten thing, what was I waiting for? Besides, I needed to hook up with him soon if I was going to invite him to the cabin.

I quietly walked up behind him, and as he paused to rest the shovel for a second, I reached around and put my hands over his eyes. It wasn't easy to do while I held a mug, believe me, but I managed.

"Guess who," I whispered, leaning closer to him.

"What the—" He wriggled to turn around, but I had him kind of stuck.

"And guess what," I said. "I made you hot chocolate!"

Suddenly he ducked, scooting out from under my arms. When he whirled around, his face expressing complete and total shock, I nearly fell over backward. "Who *are* you?" he asked.

"What are you here for?" I said. "You're—not Sean." It was the bakery guy. The Zublansky's supermarket guy. The everywhere-I-go guy.

"Nope. I'm Sean's brother." He cleared his throat. "We have this mowing and shoveling business together. Not that it's much of a business, I mean, it's really part-time and it's not like I plan to do it much longer—"

"You're Sean's *brother*," I finally murmured.

"Yup." He chipped at some ice on one square of the sidewalk, where melting ice always collected and re-froze because it wasn't quite flat. "So, is that how you usually greet Sean when he comes over to shovel the sidewalk? A little hug, a little—"

"No!" I said emphatically. "No. Not at all. Never in fact."

He gave me a suspicious look. "So what made today different?"

"I . . . well, see. . . ." This was too impossible to explain and too stupid to lie about. I'm turning over a new, um, leaf? With your brother's name on it? Ew.

"So if you don't greet Sean that way, you must have known it was me, then," he said.

"What? Shut up, I did not." I shoved him, not realizing that he was on a slippery spot and he slid backward into one of the juniper bushes, nearly landing in it.

"You're kind of a dangerous person, aren't you?" he said as I backed away, apologizing.

As Conor was getting up, I started thinking how so many things made sense now that I knew they were brothers. Why I saw them both at the skating rink that day. Why I'd bumped into Sean outside the bakery—he was probably going to see Conor. So far I'd never really seen them both in the same place at the same time, except that first day at the lake.

They were this whole Dr. Jekyll and Mr. Hyde thing. One was sweet and nice, the other gruff and insulting. And now that I knew it, I could see that of course they were brothers. They both had the same hazel eyes.

"You're not like . . . twins or something. Are you?" I asked.

"Twins? Do we *look* like twins?" he asked.

"Well. You could be fraternal twins," I said.

"No. We're hardly even related."

"Oh. You mean, you have different parents, or something?" I asked.

"No, we're just not related. In my mind, anyway." He smiled a little.

"Why do you say that?" I asked.

"My brother's okay. I wouldn't put him at the top of the family tree or anything."

"Well, no, that would be awkward, that would mean he's your great-grandfather."

His eyebrows looked slightly pinched as he thought about that.

"Sean didn't tell you about me? That I was staying here?" I asked.

He shrugged. "No."

"Oh."

"And he definitely didn't tell me you were on a hugging basis," Conor said.

"We're . . ." We're not, I was going to say, but that sounded stupid. Also, we were, some of time—at least we'd semi-hugged when we skated together. Why should I explain that to him, anyway?

But why hadn't Sean mentioned me? Maybe they weren't close. I didn't see how they couldn't be, though, considering they had to be like a year apart in age.

"You were saying?" Conor prompted as my

voice trailed off, not finishing my sentence.

"Nothing. I mean, I've gone skating with Sean. Seen him at the rink. You know, like that."

"Oh, yeah? Well, I don't usually come over here." He didn't sound happy about the fact he had to see me. "I have the other side of the neighborhood."

"Is that the good side or the bad side?" I asked.

He just looked at me for a second, as if he were making up his mind about that.

"Look. You want some hot chocolate or not?" I demanded. "'Cause it's getting cold."

"No thanks," he said. "Nice offer and all." He raised his eyebrows, and I realized that I'd been a little rude.

"Sorry. I—I guess I didn't sleep well last night."

"Yeah, I know how that is. Anyway, I have to get to the bakery pretty soon."

"Ah. Yes. The bakery." I nodded.

"You coming by later?" Conor asked, still using an ice pick to chip away the solid slippery spots. He was doing a much more thorough job than Sean had. Then again, I'd interrupted

Sean with my pajama-streaking moment.

"Maybe. I'm not sure. Kind of busy today."

"Busy?" He looked up.

"Yeah. Lots to do. Tons," I sighed. Like get over the fact I just tackled Sean's brother.

"Yeah, writing those IMs can be draining," he commented with a smile.

I couldn't stand his smug attitude. "Actually, Sean and I might be going to the Mall of America," I said.

"Ugh. What a horrible way to spend a day. A life. A couple hundred million dollars in construction."

Not that he had an attitude about malls or anything. I decided not to tell him that I kind of agreed, that I wasn't a huge mall fan, either. "So. Where's your house again?" I asked.

"Over there. See, up two blocks that way?" Conor pointed to and described a beige stucco Tudor-style house with deep red trim that sat on the corner. There was a slight curve at the end of the street, so I could see the house from the end of the driveway.

"That looks nice," I said. I stared at it long enough to commit it to memory—just in case I wanted to drop by sometime. Not that I would. Not after I'd just tackled Conor.

"Well, see you later. Have a good day."

"Yeah. You too," he said. "Look out for the Mighty Axe."

I turned around to look at him. "The what?"

"It's a ride that got stuck a few times at Camp Snoopy," he said, referring to the amusement park inside the Mall of America. "People had to hang upside down for a while. Unless you like that kind of thing."

I laughed. "Thanks for the tip."

I trudged back up to the house and let myself inside. I dumped the lukewarm hot chocolate in the sink and made myself a fresh, hot cup in the same mug. Then I collapsed into a chair at the kitchen table, where Gretchen was reading the morning paper.

"You didn't tell me that Sean had a brother. And that his brother works at the bakery," I said.

"Oh. I didn't?" Gretchen asked.

"No. You definitely didn't."

"I thought I did." Gretchen stirred a spoonful of diet drink mix into a glass of water. "Well,

I guess I thought you knew."

"Um. No," I said. "How would I know that? And you know what else? I just basically hugged—no, attacked—Conor, because I thought he was Sean."

She burst out laughing. "I know. I saw that!"

"Well, why didn't you *stop* me?" I looked out the window at Brett and Conor, who were building a snowman together.

"Actually, I didn't realize that was Conor instead of Sean until you went out there. Honestly."

"Uh huh." For some reason I didn't believe her. Now that I was looking at Conor, I could see he was a little shorter than Sean. "So what's the deal with the brothers?"

"Well. It's kind of interesting. See, Sean's like the star hockey player, star everything, in their school. But Conor isn't. I guess he was a good player, but he didn't make the team or something. Anyway, Conor is so totally jealous of Sean—you can see it. He picks fights with him all the time."

"He does?" I took that with a grain of salt. My

sister always seemed to go for the super-popular star types. It didn't surprise me that she'd like the star brother more than the other one.

Gretchen insisted on being the prom queen when she was my age. And on dating the prom king. Her ex-husband had been the senior class president at *his* school, etc. You could say she was a little obsessed with status. I shouldn't really take her advice when it came to this, in one sense. But even though her marriage had ended in divorce, she still knew a whole lot more about guys, and dating, than I did.

Of course that wasn't saying much.

"Oh, yeah. In fact they argue and fight a lot. It's hard for us to imagine, because we're so far apart in age."

"Right," I said. But I was surprised she said that it was hard to imagine. We had actually had our own share of sibling rivalry at times. I distinctly remember her pushing me aside at some extended family wedding to grab the bouquet, when she was eighteen and I was eleven. As if I *wanted* the bouquet when I was eleven!

"But the Benson boys are only one year different—"

I burst out laughing.

"What?" She stopped. "What are you laughing so hard for?"

"I'm sorry. I didn't know their last name was Benson."

"What's so funny about that?"

"The Benson boys? That's not funny to you?" I laughed again. "For one thing, you sound like Mom when you say that, and for another, the Benson boys—like they're in a band. They're not quite the Beastie Boys, but appearing tonight . . . the Benson Boys!"

"I'm done out there."

Suddenly, standing at the front door guiding Brett into the house, was Conor. There was a blast of cold air coming through the door, which was about the same feeling I got from Conor. He wasn't looking at me. He hated me. And I'd hugged him. Closely. Very closely.

I sank down in my chair a little, wishing I could disappear inside my mug as fast as the marshmallows had.

"Thanks, Conor," Gretchen said. "I was going to introduce you to Kirsten, but I guess you already met." She laughed a little. I thought about dousing her with the hot chocolate.

"Oh, yeah. We go way back," Conor said. "So, Sean will come by later if it snows any more. See ya, kid." He patted Brett on the top of his head, then he gave me a final glance, and yanked the door closed with a slam.

Okay, so we'd gotten off on the wrong foot.

I thought of the way I'd shoved him into the bushes. No, the wrong feet.

I was just getting back to the house from walking with Bear that afternoon when a small, older red pickup pulled up beside the curb. I cautiously turned to see who was stopping beside me.

Conor lowered the window on the driver's side. "Hey. I'm driving him to school hockey practice."

I peered into the cab as I walked closer.

"Coach called an extra practice because we really sucked last night," Sean said. "We lost the game and it was like the easiest team we played all year."

I walked around and leaned on the window on Sean's side. "So you can't come this afternoon?"

"No. Sorry." He sighed. "Anyway, this is my brother, Conor." He gestured with his thumb at Conor.

"Yeah. We, ah, met this morning," I said. Not to mention a couple of other times, before I knew who he really was.

"Oh, yeah?" Sean asked. "So what'd you think?"

"She thinks I'm great," Conor said. "I think she said that, actually."

Sean looked at Conor, and then at me, his eyebrows sort of semi-raised.

"I don't actually remember saying that," I said to Conor. I smiled and felt my face turn a little red.

Bear jumped up and put his paws on the window. He started panting right in Conor's face.

Conor reached down to rub Bear behind the ears. Bear pushed against him, begging for more attention.

"So which one of you is older?" I asked.

"I am," Conor said.

"Which one is taller?" I asked. "I've always been a little shorter than my sister, and it bugs me."

"I'm taller," Sean said.

"By like an inch," Conor said.

"What? I'm six-two. You're not even six feet."

"Yes I am."

"No, you're not. You're five-eleven."

"And a half," Conor added.

"It's still not six feet. So, you want to come watch practice?" Sean asked, finally turning back to me. Boy, could those two argue about nothing. Definitely siblings.

"Do you think she's stupid?" Conor asked. "Who wants to watch someone else practice?"

"We're good," Sean said.

"Not that good, if you need extra practice," Conor muttered.

"Shut up. You just wish you were still on the team."

"Well, maybe I do," Conor admitted. "But I'm sure she can think of something else to do with her time."

"Yeah. I'll probably do some reading," I said.

"Write some emails?" Conor teased.

"Maybe." I smiled.

"What's that all about?" Sean asked.

"Her project, stupid," Conor said.

"What project?"

"I told you—my Independent Study," I reminded him.

"Oh, yeah, right." Sean nodded, but I didn't think that he actually knew what I was talking about. It was okay—we hadn't discussed it much. "Okay, we should go."

"Yes, sir." Conor released the emergency brake and I laughed. He looked over at me. "What?"

"Oh. You just . . . you sort of sound like me when I talk to Gretchen."

He stared at me, as if this was highly doubtful.

"Well . . . have a good practice, Sean," I said. "Come on, Bear—let's go. See you guys later!"

When I went inside the house, Gretchen practically pounced on me. "What was that all about?"

I explained how Sean had to cancel our trip to the mall. Why I said that, I'll never know.

Naturally her response was, "Well, then, why don't *we* go to the mall?"

"Seriously? I'm not really in the mood," I said. "I have some stuff I could do here—"

"Come on," Gretchen urged. "It'll be fun!"

Somehow, with Gretchen doing all the shopping, and me entertaining Brett, I doubted that.

Maybe it wasn't too late to catch Conor and Sean.

Chapter 8

My glasses fogged over completely as I walked into the bakery the next day. I couldn't see a thing. I hated wearing my glasses when it was cold, but I'd lost a contact the day before and I didn't have a choice. I held one hand out in front of me, à la Frankenstein, so I didn't knock anyone or anything down as I slipped the glasses down my nose with my other hand.

I didn't understand how if they could come up with all these technologies for eyeglasses, like anti-glare lenses and tri-focals, and heck, laser refractive surgery, that they couldn't have anti-fog lenses.

At least I liked my new glasses. I'd picked them out before the school year and they were very cool tiny brown ovals that I personally thought looked fantastic if I wore my hair in long blond pigtails. ("Again with the Heidi look," Jones would always tease me when I did this combination, and then she'd sing, "The hills are alive . . . with the sound of music," even though that's neither Heidi nor Switzerland.)

Mom was sending replacement contact lenses from home, via overnight mail. Gretchen was home to wait for the FedEx delivery. If Mom included any baked goods by mistake, they'd be history by the time I got home. So I was here in search of sweets. I'd decided that I must have S.A.D. Not Seasonal Affective Disorder, but Sean Affective Disorder.

Not enough Sean every day.

They say one of the symptoms of S.A.D. is craving carbohydrates. Well, I definitely had that problem, and then some. I was dying for a donut. I was dying to see the sun. And I was dying to see Sean.

But since I didn't want to bowl him over any more than I already had, I'd headed to the bakery. If he happened to walk out of his house when I went past, well, great.

But he didn't.

This time, I didn't plan on staying very long, and I tied Bear to an iron bench outside the bakery so I could keep a better eye on him.

"Hey," I greeted Conor as I wiped off my glasses and waited for them to adjust to the warmer temperature indoors. "How are you?"

"Double latte," he replied, sliding a cup across the counter to me.

I turned around, expecting another customer to come up behind me. But there was no one to claim the drink.

"It's for you," Conor said.

"For me? Thanks. How did you know I was coming?" I asked.

"I saw you tying up Bear," he said.

"That's so nice of you. Thanks," I said as I slid my glasses back on, and reached for my wallet. When I looked down at the coffee, I could have sworn that the foam on top of the latte had a heart pattern. "Look! A heart," I said.

Conor was in the middle of making another espresso drink for the next customer, and he didn't look up at me. "A heart?" he said, sounding very skeptical.

"Look—in the foam," I said.

"Show me," Conor said.

"There."

"Where?"

"Hold on." I stared into the cup, turning it toward me and then back the other way. Where had it disappeared to? "It was here a second ago," I told Conor. "Shoot."

"I don't make patterns in the foam. Maybe you need new glasses?" he said.

"These are my new glasses," I said. "I lost a contact sledding with Brett yesterday."

"Oh. Well then, I don't know what to tell you." He finished making the next coffee drink and rang up the other customer's order.

I grabbed a packet of sugar and stirred it into my latte, then snapped a lid on top so that it would stay warm. I didn't care what he said. There was a heart there. Once.

"Can I get you anything else?" Conor asked.

I looked into the case, at all the pastries on trays. "How are the raspberry turnovers?"

"Not as good as the cheery cheese Danish." He pointed to a large, square pastry with cherries on top, drizzled with white icing.

"Cheery cheese? Does it smile at you?" I asked.

"I didn't say cheery. I said cherry," he insisted. "You're strange. Do you see things everywhere? Hearts, smiles—"

"You said cheery!"

"I did not. It's cherry, and you're having one." He plucked the Danish with a pair of tongs and dropped it onto a plastic, flowered plate. "On the house. How's the novel coming along?"

"Novel?"

"Whatever you call it."

"That's the thing. I need a title," I said. "So then I'll know what to call it, instead of constantly trying to explain it and failing. Like if I could think of a title that just captured the essence of it."

He didn't look impressed. I didn't expect him to be. Nothing I did seemed to make him think any more of me.

"Did that come out sounding as pretentious to you as it did to me?" I joked.

"You know, I write, too. I'm planning to

major in English or Creative Writing," Conor announced. "Unless I completely change my mind and decide to go into the forest program, which I'm also interested in. You could say I'm a little undecided, I guess."

We both laughed. "Yeah, I've got it narrowed down to English, Teaching, and ah . . ." I paused.

"Teaching English," Conor said.

"Exactly," I said. "I'm all about the teaching English. Actually, I'm thinking about law school, too."

"Really." Conor looked very surprised. "You think you could get in somewhere good?"

I wondered if he said offensive things like this to everyone, or whether it was just me. "Do you think I'm stupid or something?" I asked.

"What?"

"That's like the fourth time you've made fun of me and implied I'm not intelligent," I said. "You realize I don't have to be in school this semester because I'm basically done, too."

"Well, sure, who wouldn't be done at a school that accepts instant messages as term papers," he replied.

Ooh. He was really going for the jugular now. "Hey. It's not just IMs," I said.

"Of course not. You probably have photos and some movie ticket stubs in there, too."

I glared at him. "Could I just have my Danish now?"

"Sorry. Anyway, I thought you were here to help your sister," he said.

"I am. Does that mean I can't be working on an independent school project?" I asked Conor. "You know, you're really assuming a lot. Like, you don't even know what else I'm writing, or what I've done, or the fact I have a 4.0 average and the fact I've already been accepted to college and I have all the credits I need, so this is just for extra credit and for me personally, something I want to do."

When I took a breath, I noticed him staring at me with raised eyebrows—that look again. The one I kept getting from him when I went on one of my little tirades. "Okay. Sorry," he said. "The thing about getting in somewhere good—that was out of line."

"No, I'm sorry," I said. "It's just—it gets old when people look at me and assume I'm dumb.

I've kind of had it with that."

"Yeah. Okay." He nodded. "Consider me enlightened."

"I will." I set my cup on the counter. "Consider this a free coffee, then."

He smiled. "I will."

That night, I'd just finished tucking Brett into bed and Gretchen was about to read him a bedtime story when the doorbell rang. "That's odd," Gretchen said. "Look out the glass before you open the door, okay?"

"I always do," I assured her, trying not to get aggravated by the fact she still treated me as if I couldn't take care of myself.

"Who is it, who is it?" Brett chanted as I hurried down the stairs. Bear was barking like crazy, and racing back and forth in front of the door.

I peered through the windows and saw Sean standing on the doorstep. He waved at me, and I opened the door slowly. "Hey, what are you—"

Bear leaped at him, nearly knocking him over, then ran past him to Conor, who was standing behind Sean and holding a sled.

"Come on! Let's go sledding!" Sean cried.

Conor gave me a look, like: *I don't really want to be doing this. I was talked into it.*

I wasn't so sure I wanted to do anything with the two of them, either, considering the way they bickered. But, then again: sledding with the Benson boys? I hadn't had a better offer all year. Or all last year, either.

"Hold on—let me get my boots and coat, okay?" I pulled the door open wider. "Come on in and have a seat."

"It's okay, we'll hang out here," Sean said. "Just hurry!"

I ran to Brett's room to let Gretchen know where I was going. "Have fun. Be careful though," she said. "Don't break—"

"Anything. Anything at all," I said. I grabbed my boots, slid into them, and picked up my new, striped scarf, mittens and jacket.

"This is so great!" I said as I stepped out the door and zipped up my coat.

"You like sledding?" Sean asked.

"Oh yeah. I'm all about the sledding," I said as we started walking down the street.

"You keep saying that. How can you be 'all about' everything?" Conor asked.

I cast him an irritated glance. "I'm multi-faceted," I said. "Is that so wrong?"

"Oh, no. I'm all about being multi-faceted," Conor teased.

I ignored him and turned my attention back to Sean. "So, where are we going?"

"Minnehaha Falls," Conor announced. "They're frozen this time of year. It'll be an adventure—we'll just go sliding straight down the creek and then—"

"No, I don't think so," Sean said.

"Come on. Live a little," Conor urged him.

"No way! We'd kill ourselves," he said.

"Yeah. No kidding, genius. I was just joking," Conor said. "Just trying to liven things up. Don't worry, this hill is a little tamer than that," he said to me as he shifted the sled from his left arm to his right.

"It's a place where tons of people go, so we'll probably run into some friends," Sean said.

"Oh. Well, cool," I said.

We trekked through a couple of crusty snow drifts, then crossed Minnehaha Creek, where a small kids' bike was frozen into the ice.

"Is anyone else thinking of that Shackleton movie?" I asked.

"What Shackleton movie?" Sean asked, taking my hand and helping me up the steep bank. "Who's Shackleton?"

"You know, at the science museum last year—or was it the year before? Anyway, it was really big on TV, too. The Antarctic survival thing."

"Didn't see it," Sean said. "Never heard of it."

"You've never heard of Shackleton?" I asked. "Are you serious? Do you live under a rock?"

"He does," Conor said. "It crushed his brain."

"Shut up." Sean pushed him, and after wrestling for a few seconds, Conor went down headfirst into the snow. We left him there and kept hiking up the hill.

"I've read *Endurance*. It's an amazing story," Conor went on as he caught up to us, seemingly unfazed by being dumped into a snowbank by his brother.

The three of us stood at the top of a long hill. There were grooves in the snow from other people sledding here before us, and some large mounds that had been built up to make the sledding more exciting.

"Okay, so I just have one question before we get started," Sean said with a grin. He dropped the plastic saucer he was carrying, while Conor set down the wooden sled.

"What's that?" I asked. I figured he'd ask which way I wanted to slide—by sled or saucer.

"Do you have enough clothes on?" Sean said.

"What?" I laughed.

"I don't want you getting all frozen after we go down the hill a few times."

"Give me a break." Conor sighed loudly, disgusted by the two of us, I guess.

"You know, you can go home anytime," Sean told him.

"So can you," Conor replied.

"Shut up."

"You shut up."

Since they looked like they might start duking it out at any moment, I decided to intervene. While they were busy arguing, I molded a couple of snowballs and tossed one at each of them.

Then, once they were distracted, I hopped onto the saucer and started sliding and swirling down the hill. By the time I reached the bottom of the hill, laughing and yelling, I was turned all the way around and facing backward. I looked back up just in time to see Sean grab the sled from Conor and come hurtling toward me.

I jumped out of the way just as Sean tried to veer on the sled. He ended up flipping onto his side and coming to an abrupt stop.

"Nice driving," I teased him.

"Oh, yeah? *You* try," he replied, brushing snow off his jeans. He jogged over to me and promptly tried to stuff a handful of snow down my back.

"Nooooo!" I cried as the snow moved from my jacket collar right under my sweater and onto my skin.

"Benson! What are you doing to that poor girl?" a voice called out.

Sean turned to a group of figures heading our way in the dark. "Hey! What's up?"

"Hey, guys," Conor said as the group trudged closer.

Four guys stopped in front of us and I

exchanged an awkward smile with a couple of them.

"You going to introduce us or what?" one of them asked.

"This is Kirsten. She's visiting for a month or so," Sean explained.

"Hey," the group said, almost in unison, like they'd done this before and had a routine.

"Hi," I said with a little wave.

"How's it going?" one of them asked.

"Cold," I said. I smiled as I saw that one of the guys was pulling a long wooden toboggan.

At the top of the hill, we all piled onto the toboggan. At Sean's urging, I got on after he did, and as we shifted to get comfortable, I put my arms around Sean's waist and draped my legs over his. This was very comfortable, as far as I was concerned. A little on the outer-flirt-edge of things for me, but I could handle it.

"Room for one more," one of the guys announced.

Then Conor got on behind me.

Suddenly I was in the middle of a Benson Boys sandwich.

This couldn't be good, I thought. Then again,

it wasn't all bad. Conor kept a respectable distance, just looping his arms around my waist very loosely, and acting like he hated every minute of it. At least I knew him, so it wasn't like having one of the other guys that close to me.

We got a big push from one of the guys, and six of us went hurtling down the hill. The guy in front steered us straight over the biggest bump—and we capsized, all of us flying off into the snow.

I came down with a thud, right on top of Sean. We were lying face to face.

I smiled at Sean, who was grinning at me. Then I leaned forward and brushed his lips with a kiss.

He didn't move at first, not that he could. I pulled back for a second and looked at him. He looked a little surprised, like he wasn't sure about all this. So I leaned down to kiss him again, and he was just starting to kiss me back—

And my cell phone rang.

Cursed!

Chapter 9

$\mathcal{I}$ glanced at the caller ID though and saw that it was Jones. What was she doing calling me *now*?

"Sorry, I kind of, kind of have to take this." I smiled awkwardly at Sean, not that things could get more awkward when you were sitting on top of a boy and you'd just kissed him when you weren't sure whether that was cool or not. Although he seemed pretty cool about it, since he'd been getting into it when the phone rang.

"Where are you?" she cried when I answered.

"I'm—out," I said. *Landing on boys and kissing them!*

"Well, duh, we know you're out, silly— Emma and I are at your house looking for you! Gretchen's house, whatever."

"You *are*?" I moved aside to let Sean get up and sort of sat in the snow. He stood up and started brushing snow off of himself, then he smiled at me and started to walk back up the hill. The rest of the guys were already halfway up.

"How can you not be home? Gretchen said something about sledding. Who goes sledding anymore, I said. Get your butt over here!" Jones demanded.

"Right now?" I asked.

"Hello, we just drove two and a half hours to see you!"

I laughed. "Okay, Jones. I'll be right there." Although your timing stinks, I thought as I flipped my phone closed.

"So. Jones. Is he your boyfriend at home?" Conor asked, trudging toward me in the snow.

"What?" I asked.

"Did he drive down to see you tonight?" Conor asked.

"What are you doing, eavesdropping?" I asked.

"I lost a glove in the snow. I came back to look around for it," he said. "I heard you talking — sorry."

"Well. Not that you need to know, but Jones isn't a guy. She's Bridget, my best friend from home. She was at the rink with me that first day we met."

"We met at the lake? When?" he asked.

"You know when," I said. "You're just making me say it so that I get embarrassed all over again."

He just kept looking at me.

"I knocked you down, playing Crack the Whip. You caught me? Then you gave me back my hat?"

"Oh, yeah. Right." He grinned.

"See, you remembered all along. Anyway, Jones is a girl. Her name is Bridget, so we call her Jones. It's a book. And a movie. *Bridget Jones's Diary*?"

"Yes!" He pulled a dark-colored glove out of the snow. "Found it."

I couldn't stop glaring at him. "Look, you don't really think I'd be out here with Sean like this if I was seeing someone back home, do you?"

He shrugged. "I don't know. How should I know?"

"That is so insulting I can't even tell you. I don't have a boyfriend. I've never *had* a boyfriend, okay?" *And this conversation is getting in the way of me having one now, or ever*! I thought as I walked up the hill toward Sean.

"Well, how should I know?" Conor complained behind me. "I hear Jones, it sounds like a guy. Sue me."

"Maybe I will," I muttered as I walked toward Sean. Couldn't Jones and Emma wait another half hour until I got home? And couldn't they give me a little advance warning that they were coming? I get one fun sledding night, and they have to show up *now*?

Sean was pulling the toboggan back to the top of the hill, and I walked up beside him. He kicked a clod of snow at me, and I kicked some back.

"A friend from home just called and I have to get going — she's at the house waiting for me," I told him.

"Oh, really? That's too bad," Sean said. He didn't suggest leaving with me, and I guess I couldn't really blame him.

"You can stay," I said as I glanced at the group of his friends watching us together. "It's no problem."

"You sure?" Sean asked.

I nodded. And suddenly I couldn't wait to get out of there. The way those guys were all looking at me, like they were judging me. Had everyone seen me kiss Sean? And what did they think about it, if they had?

"Yeah—I'll be fine. See you guys!" I gave a little wave and then wrapped my scarf more tightly around my neck as I turned to walk home.

When I walked off, I heard screaming and I glanced over my shoulder to see them hurtling down the hill on the toboggan, laughing and shouting. I watched them take another huge bump and go flying into the air.

A few minutes later, I thought I sensed someone following me. It was making me really nervous. I looked back and saw a figure in the shadows. "What are you doing?"

"I just want to make sure you're safe," Conor replied, walking about ten paces behind me.

"Of course I'm safe," I said. "I'd feel a lot safer if someone weren't following me and scaring me to death."

"Sorry. But you're going the wrong way."

"I am? Shoot."

"It's this direction." He pointed to the right.

"Oh."

"Here. I'll show you," he offered. The two of us walked vaguely side by side for a while. "I have to get home to study anyway. I'm taking this lit class at the U, you know? We have an exam at the end of the week."

"Really? That's cool."

"Not really," he said.

I laughed. "The class, not the exam."

"Right." Conor coughed. "So. Are you and Sean like . . . an item?" he asked.

"I don't know. Maybe," I said.

"Can I give you a little advice?" Conor asked.

"On finding gloves in the dark? Or what?" I asked.

"Be careful," he said. "See . . . Sean has this way of drawing lots of people to him. And sometimes he hurts people when he doesn't mean to, because he doesn't realize."

"Realize what. He's popular? I think he knows that," I said.

"Look. It's not just about being popular. It's— whether he really cares about anyone, besides himself. He's incredibly selfish."

"And you're not," I said.

"Come on, Kirsten. Trust me," he said.

"Why should I trust you? Over him?"

"Because I have no reason to lie. I'm not involved."

"But he is your brother," I said. "And you are walking me home so that you can tell me to stay away from him. Which is *over*-involved, if you ask me."

"Never mind. Forget I said anything."

I could hardly look at him, I was so mad. First he thought I was rushing off to see my "hometown honey," and now what? Was he following me home to make sure I wasn't? And what was with the criticizing Sean? Brotherly love, it wasn't.

I was relieved to see Emma's car parked on the street outside Gretchen's when we got there. "That's Emma's." I pointed to the Explorer. "She's here, too." Maybe I should have had my friends come out, so I could show him that Jones was in fact a girl. But I didn't need to prove anything to him. "Emma and Jones. Best friends."

"Sounds like a musical group. Where do they live?"

"Outside Duluth, like me," I said.

"You guys have plans for the weekend?" Conor asked.

"Uh, I don't know," I said. "Why?"

"Well, we have a club hockey game tomorrow morning. Outside, down at the lake," Conor said. "It's kind of a tradition. Playing outdoors like in the old days. Sean's on one of the clubs and I'm on the other," he explained.

"Why am I not surprised?" I mumbled.

"What?"

"Nothing." Why wouldn't he come closer? He insisted on talking to me across the lawn. Was he afraid I'd tackle him again, the way I did when he came here to shovel? "I would say thanks for walking me home," I said, "but I think it's more like thanks for following me home."

"I wasn't following you," he said. "I was just being careful."

"Okay, well, whatever. Thanks," I said.

"Yeah. Have fun with your friends. Jones, Smith, Bridget Jones, whoever." Conor turned to walk home, while I laughed, opened the door and slipped inside.

"Who was that guy?" Jones asked. She completely startled me. She'd been standing by the door, watching the two of us say goodnight.

"Oh, him. He's . . . he's . . . well . . . see, sometimes he's kind of a jerk—"

"Then why are you smiling?"

Before I could answer her, Emma came clomping down the stairs in her clogs, arms outstretched for a big hug. "It's so good to see you!" she cried. "Where have you been?"

Would they even believe me if I told them I was sledding with this guy I like, and I made a move on him?

What if I told them, but it didn't work out with Sean, and then I'd be embarrassed? There was a certain humiliation factor that I had to avoid, but these were my best friends and I desperately wanted to share. "Well, see, we were sledding and . . ."

"Sledding. No wonder you're covered in

snow." Emma brushed at the back of my jeans. "You're not going to *believe* what happened today."

"No kidding! First of all," Jones said under her breath, "we've been here for half an hour already making small talk with Gretchen. She tried to serve us those nasty health crackers."

I got my secret stash of chips from the kitchen and we grabbed some cans of pop and headed upstairs to my room. Emma immediately launched into a story about how she and Cameron had a huge screaming fight in the middle of school, and how the weekend was off now, except that now Kyle wanted to take her, but she didn't really like Kyle that way except that he had given her lots of nice presents. . . .

As usual, we started inundating her with questions, and advice. Neither one asked any more about my situation.

In a way, that was okay, because I thought maybe I would ruin it by talking about it. Sometimes something so good happens that you're afraid to jinx it by saying it out loud.

❊   ❊   ❊

"Ten to one they get back together tomorrow," Jones said as she snuggled into her sleeping bag on the floor at about two o'clock in the morning. I'd given Emma my bed, and I was sacked out on an airbed beside Jones.

"Ten to one? More like one to ten," I said, and Jones laughed.

"I am so beat. I bet I fall asleep in five minutes," Jones said.

"Me too," I agreed, pulling the blanket up around my neck and adjusting the pillow.

I closed my eyes and thought about the night I'd had. I loved going sledding with Sean; even more, I loved the fact that I'd kissed him, and that he'd seemed interested.

But I couldn't get over the fact that Sean had also looked sort of stunned, as if what I did was too forward. Like we were just friends.

It wasn't as if Sean didn't enjoy spending time with me, because we'd done a lot together, and there was definitely an attraction between us. Wasn't there?

So why had he looked so surprised when I first kissed him? Was it just because all his friends were around?

I wished I could fall asleep thinking about what a great kiss it had been—because it *had* been—instead of worrying about what he thought about the kiss.

I knew what I thought about it. I wanted to kiss him again. Soon.

Chapter 10

"Didn't we meet him the last time we were here?" Jones asked as Sean skated past us at the lake, wearing full hockey regalia, passing the puck to another player.

"Didn't he kick us off the ice?"

"Not exactly," Emma said. "I think we left on our own."

I laughed. "Maybe we did, but it was strongly suggested that we take off."

We'd arrived while the hockey game was in progress, because it took us forever to get going in the morning. We sat around talking and watching stupid things on TV for too long, so we couldn't get anywhere at a decent hour. There was a fairly large crowd standing around the rink watching the game with us. A

161

chalkboard perched on a chair had the score at 1-1.

"But is that the guy who helped you up when you crashed?" Emma asked.

I nodded. "That's Sean."

"Holy cow is he good," Jones said as he skated past again. "So, is that the guy who was talking to you last night?"

I shook my head. "No, that's his brother."

"I'm confused." Emma sipped her cup of coffee. "Which one is which?"

It was hard to identify any of the players because they had so much hockey gear on, including helmets and goalie masks. "Sean's brother's name is Conor. He's playing goalie in that end. He's on the opposite club from Sean."

"That's weird," Emma said.

"They're competitive. They have what you'd call a strained relationship," I explained.

"Sounds like a lot of brothers I know," Jones commented. "So. Are they both hot?" she asked.

I laughed. "Conor is obnoxious. Conceited. Rude," I said.

"And?"

"Hot," I admitted.

She nodded and a smile spread across her face. "Uh huh. Apple doesn't fall far from the . . . tree. Or the other apples. Whatever."

Emma and I cracked up.

"So, Kirst, which one are you bringing to the cabin?" Emma asked.

I laughed. "Neither, yet! God, you guys. I barely just got here."

"Yes, true, but you've made excellent progress," Jones said. "So invite Sean already."

"I can't," I said.

"Why can't you?" Emma asked. "What if someone else asks him first?"

"No one else at home knows him," I pointed out. "How are they going to—"

"You know what I mean. He could be busy that weekend. I'd ask him, like, *today*," Emma said.

"How about now?" Jones suggested. Emma and Jones tried pushing me out onto the ice, but I pushed back, holding my ground.

Suddenly I spotted Conor. The teams were taking breaks, and he had slid his goalie mask up on his head and was looking over at us. He reached onto the top of the net for his water bottle. I waved at him, but he either didn't see me, or just wanted to act as if he didn't know me. Whatever. He was being strange, which for him, was acting in character.

"That's Conor," I explained.

"Man, you've been working hard since you got here. How many other guys do you know?" Emma asked. I'd actually managed to impress her.

"No, the question is: How many other brothers do they have, and are they our age?" Jones asked.

"Ha!" I laughed. "No, it's just the two of them."

"Okay, well, how about if you choose one and I'll take the other," Jones said.

"What *about* you? You invited anyone to the cabin yet?" I asked.

"Not exactly," she said.

"What does that mean?"

"I may have hinted at it," she said. "I may have suggested that Chris*topher* think about leaving that weekend open, just in case something comes up."

"Jones! You're mean," I said. "You shouldn't lead him on."

"I'm not leading him *on*," she said. "I may be leading him *astray*, but I'm not leading him on."

"What's the difference?" I asked.

"I don't imply anything. See, I'm inviting him as my friend, not my boyfriend. He just hasn't realized that yet."

"Well, tell him. Because I don't want to spend the whole weekend trying to cheer him up," I said.

"Of course not. You'll be busy with Mr. Wonderful."

I looked out at the ice and watched Sean skate. "February second," I murmured. "Darn. That's getting close, isn't it?"

We stood in silence, sipping our coffee and watching the game for a few minutes. I couldn't get over how good both Sean and Conor were. Sean was skating at top speed, and he made some incredibly great passes. But whenever he or his teammates made a shot on goal, Conor blocked it. Conor's team wasn't quite as good, so the puck ended up in his end of the rink more often than not.

Sean got a pass from the right wing and tried to flick the puck into the upper corner of the goal. It hit the post and bounced back, without going in. Sean jammed at it with his skates, then took a shot, his hockey stick nearly colliding right with Conor's head.

It was a goal.

It was also bloody murder.

Conor dropped his stick and they started to wrestle, pushing and shoving against each other. Conor whipped off his big, thick goalie gloves and punched Sean, just as Sean was trying to slug him.

Pretty soon the rest of the guys were involved, either fighting and punching, too, or trying to pull Sean and Conor off of each other before anyone got too badly hurt.

Watching players fight during a hockey game is not unusual. My dad always says, "We went to a fight and a hockey game broke out."

Most of the time, we'd probably applaud loudly and cheer them on—that's what we do at our high school games, especially if someone on the opposing team ends up getting both pummeled and also time in the penalty box for it.

But this was Sean. Someone was trying to punch Sean's *face*. His very nice, very good-looking face. Before my friends could get another really good look at it and be suitably impressed.

And Conor—I thought I could see that he was bleeding. And yelling. And Sean was yelling back and trying to take another swing.

"Come on, guys. Break it up, break it up!" One of the adult refs finally managed to get them apart. There was a short, official timeout, and Emma, Jones and I looked at each other uneasily.

"As I said, they're just a tiny bit competitive," I said.

"Typical," Jones sighed.

I watched Sean sitting in the makeshift penalty box (a couple of folding chairs), holding ice to his eye. Near the goal, a friend of Conor's was handing him a towel to clean off his face. Then he skated off and had to sit next to Sean.

They'd both gotten penalties for fighting.

The game continued after a brief intermission to reset the goal posts, but we spent most of the time talking, and not watching. Sean didn't score another goal, but one of his teammates did, making the final score 3-1.

"Would you guys mind going on ahead?" I asked when the final whistle blew. "I want to go talk to Sean for a sec. And I kind of want to do it in private."

"Are you going to ask him about the cabin weekend?" Jones said excitedly.

I shook my head. "Not right now."

"Why not?"

"Because—he's totally injured and I want to see if he's okay and—I'm just not." Also, because I'm petrified. Because I'm all about procrastination.

"Do it," Emma urged, giving my arm a squeeze. "We'll be waiting in the car, which is way over there." She pointed across the parking lot. "So don't sweat it, we won't be watching you and making you nervous. Take your time."

Should I ask him now? I wondered as I

started to walk over to the warming hut, where Sean had headed after the game. Maybe this was the perfect time, and not a bad time after all. He'd be extra vulnerable, what with the stitches he might need. I could drive him to the hospital. Those kinds of bonds—emotional ones, not stitches—lasted forever.

I was all smiles as I started to open the door and saw Sean sitting on the bench where he'd removed my skates when my feet were frozen solid.

Before I could step into the building, I saw a short girl with long, brown hair come up to Sean. She put her hands on his legs and leaned against him, practically crawling onto his lap. "Are you okay?" I heard her coo. And Sean smiled at her, and then she moved even closer.

Before he could see me, I let the door slam and turned around as quickly as I could.

Oh, God. "New city, new year, new Kirsten." Yeah, right. No, same old Kirsten, perpetually single. Cursed. I wasn't going to have a date for the cabin weekend. I wasn't going to have a real boyfriend, period. Ever. I started running, keeping my head down to hide how upset I was, and crashed right into someone.

"What's wrong?" Conor held my arm to keep me from falling.

"Nothing," I said.

My eyes filled with tears, which I willed to stop because I didn't want Conor to see, and I didn't want them to freeze in my eyes or on my cheeks, either. The thing that really sucks about crying in the winter is that when your tears fall, they form little icicles on your cheeks.

"Are you okay? You look weird," he said.

"Thanks. Great compliment," I said, hating my voice for being so shaky. "It's the wind, that's all. My eyes always water when it's cold and windy."

Conor hadn't let go of me yet. The next thing I knew, he leaned down from his skates-height to brush a tear from my cheek. There was a big spark when his hand touched my face, from the static electricity.

"Don't—what—" I sputtered, pulling away from him.

"I—I'm sorry. You just—you looked so sad."

"What is with you? You hate me. You do nothing but make fun of me. Now you're done beating up Sean, and you try to kiss me?"

"What are you talking about? I wasn't going to kiss you," he said. "God, you can be so vain."

"Then what were you doing?" I asked.

"You looked upset. I was trying to, like—I don't know," he said.

"Well, I don't know either. But whatever it was, forget it," I said.

"Fine. Don't feel better."

"Good. I won't!" I said. Then I wondered what I was bragging about. "See you later. No, wait. On second thought, maybe not." I darted around him and ran for Emma's waiting SUV.

Now what? The only good thing about my encounter with Conor was that it had distracted me for a second from feeling as awful as I had when I saw Sean with that girl.

The sight of the two of them came back into my mind. They'd been too close—way too close—to have been just friends. So did he have a girlfriend? Why hadn't he told me, if he did? God, how awful. No wonder he'd looked surprised when I kissed him.

"So? What happened?" Emma asked as I climbed into the front passenger seat. Jones was sprawled on the back seat, her feet up.

"Nothing," I said. This could potentially have been the biggest day of all time in my love life, I was thinking. And it was, but not the way I wanted or expected.

"Kirst? You okay?" Jones asked.

"Oh, sure. Fine." I managed a small smile.

"Did you ask him?" Emma said.

"No, I—I didn't get a chance. Too many people were around," I said. Especially the pretty one with long brown hair.

If I'd had anything to tell them about, beforehand, about me and Sean, now I wasn't sure what was going on with us. Did I have a prospect, or didn't I?

Jones leaned forward and rested her chin on the back of my seat. "I thought I saw you with goalie boy just now."

I glared at her over my shoulder. "You said you weren't going to spy."

"Sorry," she apologized.

"We were just talking. It was nothing," I said.

"Oh. Okay. Well, who's up for lunch?" Jones asked.

Somehow I couldn't imagine summoning much of an appetite.

Chapter 11

"Sean called while you were gone," Gretchen announced when I got home from lunch, and hanging out shopping with Emma and Jones. It was about five o'clock and they'd already left to go back home. "I told him you'd be home tonight, so he's coming over around six."

"He is?" I asked. The house seemed strangely empty without Brett around; he'd gone to his father's for the weekend.

"Yes. Why do you sound so surprised?" Gretchen asked.

"Because . . . I don't know," I said. I wondered if it would be possible for me to hide in my room when he came over. Probably not. What if I ran to the bathroom and pretended to be violently ill?

I just couldn't stand the thought of talking to him, after seeing him with that girl, in the warming—very warming—hut.

I'd completely made a move on him Friday night when we went sledding. Now it was Saturday night and I had no idea where we stood.

Did he want to be with me?

Or was he coming over to tell me he already had a girlfriend?

Maybe I wouldn't have to *fake* being sick. I was getting nauseous just thinking about seeing him.

When I finally focused on Gretchen again, she was staring at me. "Are you okay? You look pale."

"I'm fine," I said. "Tired, that's all."

"Come on. Let me freshen your look before he gets here." She took my arm and started to pull me toward the bathroom, where she kept a tower of beauty products. She was using one crutch to balance herself as she walked.

"What are you doing?" I asked.

"You look tired. I don't know what's going on with you guys, but you seem stressed about it. The last thing you want to do is actually let him *know* you're upset."

"I'm not upset," I said.

"What are you, then?" she asked.

I didn't want to tell her, but I had to tell someone. She knew Sean; maybe she could tell me something that made me feel better. Or maybe she knew something and wasn't telling. Either way, I had to let her know what was bothering me.

"Confused," I said.

She grabbed a compact of foundation powder and then some blush and gave me a mini-makeover while we talked. "Don't make me look too made up," I said.

"I won't," she said. "Don't worry. Now spill."

"I don't know," I said. "It's not that big a deal, I guess." I told her about the girl I'd seen with Sean, how she was all over him and how he could easily have been all over her, except that I closed the door and stopped looking.

"Oh, I wouldn't worry," Gretchen said as she leaned over to select a lipstick color for me. "That doesn't sound like much."

"It doesn't?" I said. "What if he's already seeing someone?"

"Well . . . are *you* seeing him? Technically?"

"Technically? I don't know about that," I said. "No. I guess not. I mean, we haven't known each other that long. But I felt like . . ." I didn't want to tell her about the kiss. "Like we were sort of moving that way."

"So maybe you still are," Gretchen said cheerfully. "That girl might be nothing to him. You could have interpreted the situation all wrong."

How many ways were there to interpret someone crawling on someone else's lap?

"Come on, Kirsten. Cheer up. Don't be so negative. Whatever happened, you two will work it out."

Why had I confided in her, anyway? Now she'd be giving me advice, and coordinating makeovers, on a daily basis.

"You know, you can really sound like Mom sometimes," I told her.

"I do not! God, don't ever say that again."

"Why not? You said the same thing she always used to say to me when I got in fights

177

with Tyler, or with my friends. You'll work it out. Did we ever work it out? No. It didn't work out then, and it's not going to work out now—"

"I do not sound like Mom!"

"Fine. You don't sound like Mom."

"And you are being sickeningly pessimistic," she said. "How do you know what's going on with Sean and that bimbo? You don't."

"Bimbo?" I giggled.

"Whatever. Just *ask* him. Give him a chance to explain."

Right. Just ask him. She made it sound so easy.

I thought about what I wanted to say to Sean about what I'd seen, or whether I'd say anything. For example, I could say: How could you do that to me, you pig? But he hadn't really *done* anything, except let some other girl play Florence Nightingale, instead of me. Still, I didn't like it.

The doorbell rang about half an hour later, as Gretchen and I were watching TV. I wished her leg wasn't broken so that she could get the door. But no, it had to be me.

I took a deep breath and walked over to the door.

Everything I wanted to say, or even thought about uttering, vanished completely when I saw Sean, when he smiled at me as I opened the door.

His right eye was half purple, half black and entirely puffy. He looked terrible—well, as terrible as someone as good-looking as Sean could look.

"Hey!" he said. "Where'd you go after the game? I looked for you but—"

"Oh my gosh—your eye. Does it hurt? Did you get stitches?" I asked.

"No, it's not that bad," he said. "I mean, it's not pretty. I'll give you that."

"But do you want to be pretty?" I asked. "Anyway, this will make everyone scared of you. They won't mess with you because they know you'll fight."

"Actually, this was kinda weak as far as hockey fights go. A lot of the guys have some kind of cut or missing tooth—this is nothing." Sean shrugged.

"Nothing, huh?" I stepped a little closer to

him, wanting so much to kiss his cut and make it all better—or make *me* all better, anyway. But no. That couldn't happen until I found out what was really going on.

"So where did you go?" Sean asked. "One minute you were there, with your friends at the game, and then like—you were gone."

"Well, after the fight broke out . . ." Let's see, what should I tell him. I had to escape because I saw you with someone else? And then your brother started acting strange, so . . . that was pretty much a full day?

"My friends and I went to lunch," I explained instead. "They were kind of in a hurry, so we didn't get a chance to talk to you."

"You should have called me," he said. "I could have met you guys for lunch."

He had a point. "I would have, but . . ." I was afraid you'd be out with what's-her-name hockey nurse. "We had some private stuff to talk about. Girl stuff." Normally I hate that expression, but in this case I thought it would make the topic just go away, which it did.

Sean leaned closer to me and asked softly, "Look, do you want to go somewhere?"

Yes . . . and no, I thought. I so much wanted to be close to him like this . . . but not if I wasn't the only one who got to be. "I don't know," I said.

"Just for a walk." Sean gestured to Gretchen on the sofa, watching TV. "Just for a couple minutes, so we can talk."

I nodded. "That sounds like a good idea." I grabbed my jacket from the closet by the door, and turned to Gretchen with a wave. "Be back soon!"

She smiled and gave me a thumbs-up sign. I really, really hoped Sean hadn't been able to see that.

He put his arm around my waist as we walked down the sidewalk. I could just picture us walking past his house, and Conor pelting us with snowballs.

"So. Is, um, Conor working tonight?" I asked, just to make conversation. I wasn't ready to ask the Big Question yet. Why would he have his arm around me if he wasn't into me, though?

"Probably. He's always working somewhere," Sean said.

"I noticed."

"Ever since he got cut from hockey, it's like all he does is work," Sean added.

"He got cut? Really? I thought he was so good."

"He is. But, you know. Dan is better. Trey is better. We only need two goalies."

I thought about how much that would suck, not making the team your younger brother was the star of. I knew Conor and Sean were competitive with each other. "So he plays club hockey instead?"

"Like today? Yeah." Sean nodded and gave me a little squeeze, pulling me closer. "That was some fight, huh?"

"Yeah. Does that happen a lot?" I asked.

"No. Not usually," Sean said. "Conor kept getting in my face. I was sick of it."

Conor kept getting in his face? Really? I didn't see how it would be up to Conor, considering he had to stay in the goal most of the game.

I remembered one of Jones's cardinal rules: Whenever you need to have an awkward conversation with a guy, have it outside. That way you won't have a bad association with a particular place. I waited until we turned off Minnehaha Parkway, onto a smaller street, figuring I wouldn't have to come back onto this block again.

We'd been walking in silence for a few minutes when I stopped and gently pulled myself out of Sean's arm. "Do you have a girlfriend?"

"What?" He laughed. "A girlfriend?"

"Do you?" I repeated.

"No." He shook his head. "What made you think that? Haven't you and I been sort of, like, spending time together?"

"Yeah, that's what I thought. But the thing is . . . I saw you," I said. "After the game, the fight. I came to find you, inside? And that girl had her arms around your waist and—"

"No way. We were goofing around, that's all. It didn't mean anything."

"Well, stuff usually means something. That's the thing."

"Huh?"

"I know, that sounds vague, but it's true.

Whenever you see someone kind of checking out someone else? It means they're interested. Period."

"Well, she might be interested, but I'm not," Sean said.

I didn't say anything. I wasn't convinced.

"She came in to find me. She's like—she comes to every game, she follows me around," Sean explained.

"So what are you saying? She's a groupie?"

"A what?"

"A groupie," I repeated. Sean didn't seem to know the term, though.

"She said she wanted to clean up the cut. I was wishing *you'd* come in and rescue me from *her*."

"Really?"

"Really," he said.

"Honestly."

"Yes." He held up his hand, as if he were getting sworn in. "The truth and nothing but the truth."

"She was pretty, though," I mused out loud.

"So what? You're prettier," Sean said. He put his arms around my waist and pulled me close, hugging me. "You know, I had a really good time the other night. Sledding. I wish you hadn't left, just when things were getting good."

Did he mean the kiss? Or the toboggan rides? Because when I left, he was hanging out with his friends, not me.

But how could I hold that against him? I was the one who'd answered my cell phone while we were kissing. If anyone had been rude, it was me.

"Me, too," I said. "I'm sorry I took off. But Emma and Jones showed up, and I had to meet them."

"It's okay. I understand."

"You do?"

"Yeah."

"But . . . do you understand why it looked kind of bad, when I saw you with . . . what was her name?" I asked.

"Melissa. She . . . really, she's not my girlfriend."

I looked into his eyes. He seemed completely honest. Not to mention completely hot.

Sean pulled away and looked at me. "Hey, I've been thinking."

"What?" I was filled with anticipation.

"You want to go to Buck Hill after all?" he said.

That wasn't exactly the sweet romantic thing I'd been waiting for him to say, but it wasn't bad.

"Sure! Anytime," I said. But I got this picture of me with my skis crossed, butt up, face down, in the snow. Then, the next day, Gretchen and I sitting on the sofa, side by side, staring out the picture window, waiting for something interesting to happen, for someone to fall on their way past. Spring would come and we'd still be there, immobilized, and both on diets . . .

"There's this charity event on Presidents' Day," Sean continued. "Tons of high schools participate. It's a mattress race."

I coughed. "Excuse me?"

"Teams wear costumes and have themes and stuff. You slide down on a mattress, or on cardboard boxes, or on whatever you've made. We've all collected pledges at school. They give out awards for best costume, most money raised, all that."

"Isn't your mattress . . . full already?" I

asked, picturing Sean's group of friends all piled on top of it.

"We need a girl," he said.

I bet, I thought.

"Our theme is Snow White and the Seven Hockey Players."

I couldn't even begin to think about how dumb that sounded. But then, a mattress race already sounded pretty stupid, on its own. "You're kidding."

"No." He laughed. "But Snow White dropped out. She was dating Ian, but they broke up, so we're, like . . . well, we're sort of screwed. Please say yes."

"Doesn't some other girl at school want to do it?" I asked.

"Maybe. But who cares? I want *you* to do it," he said. "And hey, if it sucks, we could just do this." He kissed me, pulling me toward him. Then suddenly he was pushing my hair back behind my ear and saying, "Okay, got to go. Call me tomorrow—we'll hang out."

I was in kind of a daze as I watched him jog down the street toward his house.

As I walked into the house, I thought: *I*

should have invited him to the cabin just then. I'd missed a totally perfect opportunity. What was my problem?

I was so happy that I didn't even mind being sent to buy groceries by Gretchen as soon as I got home and told her everything was okay. She was smart enough not to say "I told you so," which helped.

I didn't see Conor when I walked into Zublansky's, so I figured he wasn't there. I grabbed a basket and walked around quickly to collect the stuff we needed for dinner. As I stepped up to Lane 8 to check out, suddenly Conor appeared.

"I've got it," he volunteered, walking over to the line where I was standing. "Paper or plastic?" he asked me.

"Plastic," I said.

"How's it going?" He tried to sound casual, but his voice sounded a little forced to me. *He could have avoided this—and me,* I thought. Considering the way we'd left things earlier in the day, that's what I would have done. So why was he jumping over to my line to help me?

I noticed he had a bruise near his eye, like Sean. "Ouch. Your face doesn't look too good either," I said.

"Excuse me?"

"No! I mean, your face is fine, your face is great. Just a little beat up."

"It's nothing. It doesn't hurt. Superficial scrape is all. What's for dinner tonight?" Conor asked as he started to pack the groceries.

"Chicken."

"Yeah. I kind of figured." He dropped the package of chicken into a plastic bag and it landed with a loud thump.

"Easy. Don't break the chicken," I said.

"I think it's been broken already," he said dryly. "So, just chicken. Baked? Fried?"

"Chicken with onions, mushrooms, peppers and tomatoes," I said.

"No kidding," he commented as he bagged each item in the same order I listed it. He stopped when he got to the tomatoes, and shook the plastic bag so that three of them rolled out. He started to juggle them, saying "I'm all about the tomatoes."

The cashier and I looked at him, and then at

each other, and exchanged irritated, he-is-so-annoying-and-we-have-no-patience-for-this glances.

When he dropped one tomato, he swore, then quickly let the other two fall right into a waiting plastic bag. "So, Italian night or what?" he asked.

"I don't know what we're having, actually. It's Gretchen's list, but I'm guessing it's some kind of Italian dish. If you must know."

"Oh, I had to know. I'm very nosy when it comes to my customers' meal planning."

"You are?" I laughed.

"No, not usually. People buy stuff that you don't even want to think about putting together for a meal."

"Like what?" I asked.

"Like . . . prunes and ground beef," he said. "Lots and lots of both." He made a face.

"Conor," the cashier, an older woman, said in a weary, warning tone. "More bagging, less commentizing."

"Commentizing?" Conor dropped a loaf of Italian bread and a package of thin spaghetti into a new plastic bag. "Mary, you are making up new words every day."

"I have to do something to amuse myself," she said. "You sure don't help."

"Help? Did you say help?" Conor cleared his throat. "Yes? Okay. I'd be glad to help you, Miss," he said in a loud voice.

"*Miss*?" I repeated as I followed him out the automatic doors, past a bunch of giveaway newspapers in wire displays and a collection of carts and baskets. "Since when am I a Miss?"

"What do you want to be? Ma'am?" He quickly wheeled the metal cart toward the door.

"How about just . . . how about you let me carry my own bags?" I said.

"We have a rule here. Two bags' worth, and you get me," he said.

"Remind me to shop lightly next time, then," I said. "Anyway, what's in that bag? One thing?"

Conor laughed and strode out the automated exit doors ahead of me. "I wanted some air, okay? It gets boring in there." He turned to the left as we headed across the parking lot, just as I turned right.

The cart smashed into my shin, then its

wheels rolled right over my foot. "Hey! Watch it!" I cried. I jumped back out of the way, and Conor stopped in the middle of the lane to apologize.

"Look out!" I said, pushing Conor as a car came toward him, and he grabbed the cart to catch his balance.

The car veered around Conor—and instead sprayed *me* with slush as it went past.

"You are a seriously dangerous person. You know that?" Conor commented as he wheeled his way out of the driving lane.

"Hey. I'm the one who just got her foot run over. Not to mention drenched." I looked at the bottom of my jeans, which were now soaked with water and slush.

"Like it hurt. There's nothing in this basket," Conor said as we started to move toward the minivan again.

"Then why are you carrying it out for me?" I asked.

"I told you! I wanted some air. Do you know how boring it gets, arranging things in geometric shapes in bags?" he asked.

I laughed. "Well, enjoy the fresh air. By all

means." I lifted the back of the minivan and he put the grocery bags inside, even though I could have done it myself with no problem. I hoped he wasn't expecting a tip.

"Well, thanks," I said, closing the hatch.

"No problem. Sorry about your foot," Conor said.

It was hard to take him seriously when he was standing there in an apron. "You should take some time off or something," I said. "You work too much."

"Oh, yeah? This, coming from someone whose idea of work is collecting text messages?" he scoffed.

How could one person be so nice, and so rude, at the same time? "Okay, well, *bye*," I said. "Have a great night."

Well, at least I didn't have to worry about what had happened that morning. Things with Sean were fixed, and fine. Things with Conor were back to normal: in other words, strange.

Chapter 12

"*E*xcuse me," I said as I climbed into the small, red pickup truck. "But what are you doing here?"

Shouldn't you be at work? I wanted to say. *A double latte goes unmade right now because of you.*

"Ask him." Conor didn't look thrilled as I scooted over across the bench seat to sit next to him. Sean climbed in after me and slammed the door closed.

"Don't slam it," Conor said, aggravated. He looked like he needed a few more cups of coffee or something. I remembered Paula saying that he wasn't a morning person.

"I didn't slam it," Sean protested. "I *closed* it."

I sat there between the two of them: Conor

was behind the wheel, my left leg was jammed against the shift-stick, and Sean was as close as he could be to my right leg. The mattress for the charity event was tied to the roof, on the truck topper.

"He insisted on driving when Ian couldn't get the car like he thought," Sean explained.

"I didn't want to drive," Conor said. "You made me."

"No, you just didn't want *me* to drive your truck," Sean replied.

"Exactly."

"So. Nice weather today," I said, trying to interrupt before they turned this into a full-scale, all-day argument. "Sunny, not too cold . . ."

"Believe me, there are things I'd rather be doing," Conor mumbled.

"No doubt," Sean said. "Like harassing someone else?"

We pulled out of the neighborhood and started heading down Interstate Highway 35. If we took this highway north, we'd end up back at my hometown. Which maybe wasn't such a bad idea, with things going so strangely this morning. But we were going south.

I was completely confused by the Benson Boys.

First, one of them basically starts dating me and we kiss. But then I see him with another girl. He says it's nothing, but I'm worried. And we kiss some more.

Second, the other one acts like he thinks I'm stupid. Then all of a sudden he starts following me everywhere. Then he almost sort of kisses me.

And now here I was, smushed between the two of them, with a mattress bouncing on the rooftop, being buffeted by the wind as we reached sixty miles an hour.

Conor accidentally put his hand on my leg as he reached to push the stick shift into overdrive. "Oh, sorry," he said, turning to me with a bashful smile.

"Sorry," Sean muttered. "You're not sorry. Well, you are, but not that way." Then he snuggled closer to me, and put his hand on my other leg.

I wondered how far away this Buck Hill

place was, and whether we'd all survive the journey intact.

When we reached the ski area, we had to park at the outskirts of the lot because we were a little on the late side. Conor and Sean hoisted the mattress off the truck and carried it on their heads over to the staging area, near the rope tow.

A local radio station was sponsoring the event, along with several other businesses. They had tables set up and were selling T-shirts to raise money. Music was blasting from speakers on top of a black van. There must have been a few hundred kids milling around, some in costumes and some as spectators, and lots of parents, too.

When we went up to the table to register, I wandered up and down the line, checking out the other organizations there.

"Are you going to sign up for the loppet?" Conor asked as he and Sean came up behind me.

"No. What's a loppet?" I said.

"A ski race," Conor said. "It's Norwegian.

This one's in Mora and it's called the Vasa-loppet—it's 30K."

"Oh. Well, then I don't think so," I said. "I've never really done much cross-country skiing before. I tried telemarketing once—"

"Telemarketing?" Conor burst out laughing. "Did you say 'telemarketing'?"

"What," I said.

"I think you mean telemarking," he said.

I grinned. "Oh yeah. That sounds better."

And everyone at the table started laughing at me, and both Sean and Conor were laughing, too. The one time they agreed on something, and it had to come at *my* expense.

"Yeah, that's the worst kind of skiing," Conor said. "You have to hold the phone to your ear while you're going downhill. There's the do-not-call list, and then there's the do-not-fall list," Conor added.

"Very funny," I said. But I couldn't stop myself from smiling, because it actually was.

"I'm going to go find the guys—we're meeting over by the locker room. I'll be right back with your costume," Sean said. "Ian's bringing it."

After he jogged off, Conor and I stood there for a minute, looking around at all the other contestants—if that's what you would call them. "Don't you need to find your team?" I asked him.

"Oh, no. I'm not doing this," he said.

"Why not?"

"Are you serious? I'm just here to laugh at everyone else."

"Why? Is there going to be a lot to laugh about?" I asked.

"Yeah. I think so," Conor said. "For example? Here come the seven idiots."

Sean and his friends were walking toward us. Their costumes were simple, no-brainers: They wore hockey team jerseys, over jeans. Some of them wore ball caps. A few of them carried hockey sticks.

"Hey," a few of them greeted Conor, and me. As they all gathered around me, all I can say is that one or more of their shirts definitely hadn't been *washed* since the last game. Which I guess made it an authentic costume.

"Which one's Dopey? That you?" Conor asked Sean.

"Ha ha," Sean muttered. "Look, Conor, you've got to help us out."

"Wait a second. I only count six hockey players," I said.

"Exactly. That's why you've gotta do it with us, Conor," Sean said. He held out a jersey. "Tommy's sick. You have to fill in for him."

Conor stared at the jersey. "You want me to wear the sick guy's jersey?"

"It's not Tommy's, it's one of mine," Ian said. "I brought an extra after he called to say he couldn't make it."

"Go change," Sean said.

"Wait. Who said I was doing this?" Conor said as he caught the jersey Ian tossed to him.

Then Sean held out a sparkling tiara to me. "Here's your crown."

"Snow White wore a crown? Really?" I asked. I put it on top of my head and mashed it down so that it would stay there. "Okay, that was easy. I'm ready!"

"And . . . here's your outfit." Ian handed me a black garment bag.

"Oh." I peeked at the dress inside. I nearly dropped it. The costume looked like it might fit someone half my height. I held it up against me. "You cannot be serious. This is going to be way too short on me!"

"Hey, maybe we'll score more points with the judges." Sean winked at me, and his friends laughed.

I don't want to score more points with the judges, I thought. *I really only want to score points with you.*

Therefore, I'd wear the outfit.

"Be right back," I told the guys. Unless of course I ditched this entire event and ran for the hills. There were lots of hills around. It wouldn't be hard.

"You have to be kidding me. This whole thing makes no sense," I muttered as I changed into the outfit in the women's locker room. Fortunately there were a few private changing rooms so I didn't have to try it on in front of everyone. "Since when did Snow White hang out with hockey players?"

This must be what's known as "taking one for the team," I thought as I examined the skimpy cocktail-waitress-type outfit. It must have been from some sexy costume shop. Or sex shop, rather.

There was a short black skirt—a mini—and a white blouse that cinched right below the bust line. I was a Vegas act waiting to happen. I slipped my pink, furry boots back on, to keep my legs warm. Then I put on some deep red lipstick I'd borrowed from Gretchen for the part, and fixed my hair with the tiara. Wasn't Snow White a brunette? And I was pretty sure she didn't parade her cleavage around town. But oh well. This was for Sean.

I put on my jacket and stepped slowly out of the locker room. A couple of girls gave me critical glances, and I winced. Why am I doing this? I wondered. No wonder that other girl dropped out. She probably saw the costume, then changed her mind.

When I finally met up with Sean, he was waiting anxiously for me. "Come on, they're all waiting at the top. Our start time is in fifteen minutes," he said.

He didn't even bat an eyelash at the fact I was all legs. Did this not faze him? Or was I not impressive as a leggy fairy tale heroine?

On our way up the ski lift (and I don't even want to think of the view from below), a team went by on its way down in a cardboard ship that said, "Pirates of Lake Minnetonka." A guy who looked a lot like Captain Jack Sparrow was at the helm, while ghosts—some real, some made of sheets—bobbed behind him.

Couldn't I have been on *that* mattress ship? *I'd kill to be a ghost right now*, I thought. *No pun intended.*

We got to the top of the hill, and I saw the mattress and its pseudo-platform that I was supposed to lie on. It looked like an old desk with a few sleeping bags piled on top of it. Whatever these guys ended up doing with the rest of their lives, you can bet it wouldn't be construction or design. One of them handed me a clump of plastic flowers to hold.

When the M.C. introduced our group, the guys raised their hands over their heads, like victorious boxers, and everyone cheered.

"You have to take off your coat," Sean told me as he bowed to the crowd.

"I think she should keep it on," Conor argued.

"I'm with you," I said to Conor. I wasn't about to do *any* bowing, needless to say.

"Come on, Kirst. Let 'em see the costume, or

it won't count," Sean urged.

"Okay, fine." I kept my jacket on until the last second. Then I flung it over to the side, and stood there awkwardly grinning and waving at the crowd. Meanwhile, the rest of the team was standing there sort of gaping at me.

We all gathered on the mattress, me lying on the platform and the guys standing around me, sort of in surfing stances.

"Whose bright idea was it to put non-stick Pam on the bottom of the mattress again?" someone asked Sean as we began hurtling down the slick snow.

"Come on, this is fun!" Sean cried.

Needless to say, we lasted about halfway down the steep hill. Guys tumbled off, or dropped to their knees to stay on. We were setting some kind of land speed mattress record, that was for sure.

At the bottom, we crashed into the hay bales and everyone tumbled on top of me, especially Sean. It was almost just like when we rolled off the toboggan, except this time I had less clothes on. Funny things happened when we went down slopes together.

Conor was one of the first people to get up. He leaned down to help pull me to my feet. "Come on, get up, your fans await."

A huge cheer went up from the crowd gathered to watch, as we untangled ourselves, all stood up, and stepped off the mattress.

"Skirt," Conor said out of the corner of his mouth.

I reached back and realized that my skirt had flipped up in the back. I pulled it back into place and muttered, "Thanks."

Then the guys surrounded me, and we all posed for pictures. I didn't think we'd win any prizes for that performance, but at least we'd raised money for charity. Gretchen had kicked in fifty dollars when I told her about the event.

"Do you want to go get a hot chocolate or something?" I asked Sean as we moved out of the way, so the next team could come down the hill. *And some clothes? For me? Please?*

"Sure. But I want to go down the hill a few more times—maybe jump on someone else's ride," Sean said. "Don't you?"

"Not without changing first," I said. "Are you crazy?"

"Crazy about that costume," Sean said. "Can I call you 'Snow' from now on?"

"I'm contemplating suing you," I said through clenched teeth as we posed for yet another photograph. "These photos. You're going to confiscate them, right?"

"Oh. Right. Sure." From Sean's reaction, I wasn't sure if he knew what "confiscate" meant.

"Okay, now I really must go." I tried to give him a kiss on the cheek, but he turned away to talk to some pals just as I was leaning toward him, and I ended up kissing the air instead.

I walked as inconspicuously as I could away from the stage area, making sure I didn't take any long strides that might make my costume ride up—again.

Conor was waiting off to the side with my jacket, which he must have carried down from the top. "Thanks," I said.

"Hold on." Then he thought better of it, and took off *his* jacket to give me, because it was longer and would cover more of me.

"Thanks, but I'll just go change," I said. "I'm ready to turn into a different fairy-tale character."

"Yeah, me too," Conor agreed as we started to walk up toward the lodge.

Suddenly a couple of guys stepped in front of us—they looked like they were about twenty. "Hey, Snow White! Can I be your prince?" one of them asked.

I would have killed for my over-protective dad to show up right about then. Fortunately, this was something I could deal with on my own. "I don't think so," I said firmly.

"Come on," the other guy said. "Aren't we supposed to kiss you to wake you up?"

"Yeah. In your dreams," I said. I started to walk past them, and one of them reached out to put his arm around me.

I jammed him in the ribs with my elbow, dodged out of the way, and said, "Leave me alone, or I'll have the seven hockey players find you. They carry hockey sticks, okay?"

I heaved a sigh of relief once I was back into my own clothes—jeans and a sweater. My furry boots looked much better with jeans than they did with a mini. I hung up the Snow White costume and put it back into the garment bag, then draped it over my arm and walked back to the lodge lounge.

Conor was waiting outside the entrance. "You're funny. You know that?"

"What?"

"You nearly knocked that guy out!" He laughed. "So, you going to go with the tiara for the rest of the day?"

I'd put it back on after I changed clothes, because I didn't have a good place to set it. Then I'd forgotten all about it. "Oh. Oops." I reached up and started to take off the tiara, but then I thought better of it. Maybe everyone would treat me like a princess if I acted like one. "Actually, yes."

"Okay . . ." he said slowly.

"I think I'm going outside to watch," I announced.

"You don't have to." Conor pointed to the video screens around the lounge. Tons of other people were hanging inside and watching by camera. "I mean, if you don't want to put your hat on over your tiara."

"That could be lumpy. I don't know. I should go find Sean, though," I said.

"Found him." Conor pointed to a large video screen on the wall. Sean was cruising down the mountain on a mattress decorated to look like an MTV Spring Break party, complete with girls in bikinis and guys in shorts, dancing in his jeans and T-shirt.

"Oh. Well, that looks like fun. Sort of." As long as I didn't look at the bikini-clad girls getting really close to Sean.

Conor shook his head. "He'll do anything for attention."

I turned to him. "Okay. I have a question. Do you guys really not get along, or is it all an act? I mean, I don't get it, Conor."

"It's kind of a long story. I'll buy you a coffee," he offered.

We settled onto a couple of stools at the bar, and I ordered a mocha while Conor got a plain black coffee.

"Okay." Conor sighed. "It's stupid."

"So tell me how stupid," I insisted as I checked out the big-screen TV on the wall.

Fortunately Sean wasn't on screen anymore.

"I quit the hockey team last year and he's still mad at me about it, because they lost in the tournament."

"You quit?" I asked. "I thought you didn't make the team."

"No, that's true, too. I didn't make it this year—this fall," Conor said. "I wanted to get back on the team, but the coach didn't want me back. I guess I can't really blame him. He didn't trust me."

"Why not? When did you quit?" I took a sip of the café mocha.

"Just before the tournament."

"No. Why would you do that?"

"Yeah, I know, believe me, I've had tons of time to think about what a dumb move that was. It was impulsive. It was awful of me to do that to those guys. But I couldn't stand them anymore. They're egomaniacs."

"Come on. We have star hockey players at our school, too. They're nice, mostly."

"I know, I know. It's not like the norm— I'm not saying that. It's just, at our school, Sean and his buds are the jocks you have to

follow around and bow down to and it's just —
you know, it's crap."

I laughed. "Crap?"

"Yes. The things they do when they're off
the ice, I don't know, I guess it's all part of high
school. And I basically hate high school right
now."

"Why?"

"Because. It's so fake. It's so competitive. I
hate cliques," Conor said.

"Oh. Is that all?" I asked.

Conor frowned. "You don't know what it's
like to be compared to Sean all the time."

"No, I don't. I mean, that would be weird,
right?" I asked, trying to lighten the mood. "For
one thing, he's taller. For another, he's a guy."

He didn't smile.

"Maybe it sucks to have a star for a brother.
But you're just as talented as he is, right? You're
a great goalie. Even Sean said that."

"He did?" Conor seemed surprised, as if he
didn't expect Sean to be able to say one nice
thing about him. Even if that were true, in
reverse. "Yeah. Well, goalies don't have the same
star power," he said. "We have great speed, great

reactions, great hand-eye coordination. But no groupies."

I smiled, thinking of how when I'd asked Sean about that brown-haired girl being a groupie, he hadn't seemed to know what that meant. "You know what? I tried hockey once," I said.

"Yeah?"

"Yeah. Field hockey. In PE class. Hated it," I said. "Broke my best friend's finger, too."

"How'd you manage that?"

"I hit her with the ball," I said. "I was, I don't know, taking a slap shot I guess. And the ball hit her stick and instead of stopping it, she somehow let it run up the stick and jam her finger dead-on."

"That's hilarious," Conor said. "You flattened her finger enough to break it?"

"She was cursing so loudly that we both got detention for a week. But that's Jones. You know, Jones. The *girl*," I said.

His face turned slightly pink. "So, what position did you play in field hockey?"

"I don't remember exactly. Fullback, maybe? I was supposed to stop people from getting to the goal. Yeah, that was it. Fullback."

He was just looking at me.

"I didn't stop anyone," I said. "The goalie hated me."

"Well. Don't worry. Not all goalies hate you," he said.

We exchanged this really awkward smile.

"Well, good," I said. "I guess."

About an hour later, Sean and I were sitting in front of one of the fireplaces in the lodge. We were snuggled together on a sofa, and I was leaning back against him.

Forget about coffee. We'd moved on to hot chocolate. We'd moved on to getting whipped cream on our lips and kissing it off, and other disgusting public displays of affection like that.

"So you like this kind of stuff. Right?" I asked Sean, looking up at him over my shoulder.

"This kind?" Sean snuggled closer to me and kissed my neck. "Yeah."

"No, I mean . . . I meant . . ." It was hard to concentrate when he was doing that. "Ski trips and skiing and trips and stuff."

"Of course," Sean said, running his hand down my arm, tracing the stripe on my sweater sleeve. "Winter Carnival is coming, you know?"

I nodded. "I'm really looking forward to it. My friends are coming back to visit then."

"Well, there's this big party at my friend's house, over in St. Paul every year during Winter Carnival. It's called the Snow Ball. It's a formal," Sean explained. "It's a little over the top—like you're forced to dress up—but they usually have a band, and great food, and lots of kids from school go."

"Uh, is it always called the Snow Ball?" I asked.

"As far as I know. Anyway, it's over in St. Paul, in a huge house on Summit. Like, a mansion. So. It would be really cool if you'd go with me."

"Sure," I said. "I'd love to! But, uh, I was about to ask you something. So how about . . . well, I'll make you a deal."

"Oh, yeah?" Sean asked. "What kind of deal?"

"I'll go to the Snow Ball with you, if you'll

come away for Groundhog Day weekend with me."

"Come away for the weekend? Where?" He seemed really nervous all of a sudden.

"Look, relax, it's no big deal. I'm not talking about you coming to meet my parents or anything." I laughed. "It's a ski weekend with my friends—a bunch of us are renting a big cabin up north."

"Oh. Well, that sounds cool. Yeah. I think I could probably go. I'll have to make sure I don't have a game or anything. I might have a game."

How many times was he going to say that? "Of course, right. I didn't think of that. Well, you can at least come for part of the weekend. It's a long weekend because there's a school holiday and . . ." *And it's the least you could do for me, considering I went sliding down a hill as a tarted-up Snow White for you!* I thought.

"So, you will come, right?" I pressed Sean.

"Definitely. As long as I don't have to be here for hockey."

Suddenly Conor was standing in front of us, blocking our view of the fire, blocking the entire fireplace, blocking the *sun* even. "Let's get going," he said. "I have to get to work."

And even though Sean and I protested for about three minutes, it was useless, and ten minutes later we were heading back to the Cities together, jammed into the pickup all over again.

Chapter 13

"Okay, I did it!" I told Jones when she answered the phone later that night. "I officially have a date for Groundhog Getaway. At least I think I do."

"Yes! That's awesome," she said. "Who with?"

"Sean, who do you think?" I said. I described the strange chain of events that had led to the invitations on both sides.

"Snow White, huh? You know what? If I were you, Snow, I'd have a back-up plan," Jones said.

"What?" I asked. "Why would you say that?"

"The guy sounds a little flaky to me. He just asked you to this dance that's, like, in two weeks. I'm just wondering—all that stuff you told me about whether he might have a game or not.

What about that brother of his? Didn't he get cut from the team, and therefore has no game? Which isn't to say that he doesn't have game. He's got game."

I laughed.

"In fact, if you're not going to ask him to Groundhog Getaway, then maybe I will," Jones mused.

"What? No way!" I said.

"Why not?"

"Because. You don't even know him," I said.

"So? You know him," she pointed out. "And even though you don't like him sometimes, he does make you laugh. I saw you laughing that one time. And what better date could there be for an entire weekend, but someone who can really make it fun—"

"Jones?" I interrupted. "You're really getting carried away with this," I said. "You're not asking Conor."

"I'm not?"

"No!" I said, my reaction a little stronger than I expected.

"And why not?" Jones said.

"Because!" Wasn't it obvious? "I'm . . . I'm

bringing Sean. And they don't get along very well, so it wouldn't work."

"Oh. Well, okay. Geez, Kirst. I was only *joking*. You really flew off the handle there for a second."

"Sorry," I said. "I'm—I guess I'm excited about going and it's just coming out wrong."

"Okay. So Conor's out. No problem. Who else have you met down there? Anyone who looks like Topher?"

We both started to laugh, and I had time to think about why I'd just reacted that way. I liked Conor, sort of; so why *couldn't* he go with Jones? Wouldn't they make a good couple, sort of?

What was my sort-of problem?

It was almost like I was more interested in taking Conor to the cabin with me, than Sean. But that didn't make any sense. Sean was the one I had chemistry with; the one I'd kissed; the one who'd pursued me ever since I got to town, and vice versa.

I didn't want to go out with Conor instead of Sean. I just didn't want anyone else to go out with Conor, either.

I couldn't wait to see Sean. That's what I was
thinking as I marched to the rink at the lake a
few days later. Bear was pulling me at top speed,
and I didn't care—I wanted to sprint down
there. I was half-running, half-walking.

I'd called Sean's house, and his mother told
me he'd be at the lake after school.

When I got there, the ice was nearly empty.
Hardly anyone else was crazy enough to be out
on a day like this. It was like negative thirteen
degrees and windy.

I went into the warm-up room and shivered
by the heating vent for a few minutes. A few
moms with young kids were inside, trying to
warm up by sipping hot chocolate from
Thermoses.

When Conor opened the door to the building,
we both totally flinched. He obviously hadn't
been expecting to see me, and vice versa. I hadn't
seen him since the day of the Snow White
escapade, when we'd had a semi-normal time
together, talking.

"Hey. What's up?" I asked.

"Not much," he said, hopping up onto the

table and dropping his duffel bag onto the floor. He was dressed in full goalie gear, except for the leg pads, which he started to fasten now as he talked to me.

"Nice day out," I commented. "If you like ice cubes."

"Oh, yah. Super," he said, imitating a heavy Minnesotan accent. "Sorry, my grandfather came over for breakfast this morning. He thinks everything is super. Super, ya. You busted out your knee tending goal last night, then. Super."

"You betcha?" I asked.

He grinned. "Exactly."

"I hate that stereotype, but sometimes it's just true, right?" He nodded. "So, did you bust your knee?" I looked at his legs, and he didn't seem to have any bandages.

"No, my knee's fine," Conor said. "It should be in great shape by the time baseball season starts."

"You play baseball?" I asked. "What position?"

"Catcher," he said.

"Cool. I'm on the softball team," I said. "I play first base."

"No kidding. I wouldn't have guessed," he said.

"Why not?"

"'Cause I'm stupid, I guess. I thought maybe Sean would have mentioned it."

"He, um, never asked either, but I think I told him," I said. "Sean around, by any chance?" I finally asked, in as casual a tone as I could muster.

"Yeah, he's out there."

"Oh, good," I said, just as I heard Bear bark a few times. "And Bear needs me, so . . . I'll see you out there, okay?" Outside, I stopped to rub Bear behind the ears. I unclipped his leash from the bench where I'd tied it, and we started to walk over toward the rink where Sean and some other guys were practicing by taking shots on goal.

Bear lunged forward, pulling me with him. Sean noticed me then, and waved with his hockey stick. He started to skate over toward us, and Bear started to run toward him, dragging me onto the ice.

My feet went out from under me, and I fell

backward. I slammed onto the ice, the back of my head hitting it kind of hard.

As I sat up, embarrassed, I thought I saw a few stars floating around my head, the way they do when you stand up too quickly.

Sean came up and his skates sprayed me with ice shavings as he came to a stylish stop right in front of me. Conor, of course, was already there, and Bear was running in circles around me and barking, to attract even *more* attention.

Conor took one of my arms, while Sean took the other to help me to my feet. "Hey, Kirsten! You okay?" Sean asked.

"Oh, yeah. Fine," I said as I brushed a little snow off my jeans.

"You're okay? You sure?" Conor asked, touching my elbow.

"Yeah, I'm fine."

I know they both talked to me for a few minutes after that, but the next five minutes were actually sort of a blur. More guys showed up to play, and I stood there watching the game for a while, but then I realized not only was I cold, my head was starting to hurt from where I'd whacked it on the ice, and I didn't really care about hockey right now, or who won or lost the game.

As I was walking home, Conor pulled up beside me in that old pickup of his. "Kirsten? You want a ride?" he asked.

"I'm almost there," I said.

"Well, actually . . . you're not quite there. You're a little off course. I've been looking all over for you for the past twenty minutes."

"Oh." No wonder Bear had been trying to drag me in the other direction. He knew the way back to Gretchen's better than I did.

Conor got out of the truck and he was still in his hockey gear, all his pads. He had socks on but no shoes, and his goalie mask was sitting on the dashboard.

"Don't you have to get back to the game?" I asked as he helped me into the passenger seat. Bear hopped onto my lap, which wasn't exactly an easy fit. He weighs about eighty pounds. If my head wasn't hurting, my legs would soon.

"No. I mean, the guys might think so, but it's not that important to me right now. I'm kind of more worried about you," Conor said.

"I'm fine," I said.

"I don't know if you are," he said. "Anyway I have a history of ditching, so people pretty much expect it of me at this point." He smiled as he pulled into our driveway.

Bear and I got out of the truck and I pulled the house keys out of my pocket. I unlocked the front door and walked into the house. Conor was following right behind me.

"So are you really feeling okay?" he asked.

"Yeah. I have a headache, but . . ."

"I'm kind of worried you might have a concussion," he said. "Maybe I should take you to the doctor."

"What? Are you crazy?" I asked. "I'm fine. Really."

"Well, I don't want to leave you here alone," he said.

"Gretchen's around here somewhere. She hardly ever leaves. Unless I want to leave, and then she's gone, history, see you," I muttered.

"Gretchen!" Conor called around the house, and his deep voice startled me.

"Where is Gretchen?" I muttered. "Oh, yeah.

Brett's at a friend's house, and Gretchen went out with her friends. She said she'd be back late. Ish."

"Ish? Do you feel nauseous?" he asked. "Should I get you to the bathroom—grab a trashcan?"

"No. Late-ish, she said."

"Oh." He laughed. "Okay, well, why don't you sit on the sofa. I'll get you a glass of water." He turned on the fireplace and went to the kitchen.

"So. Your name and date of birth are?" he asked as he returned.

"Come on, I'm not that out of it." I watched the flames dance in the fake fireplace.

"Still. Just tell me," Conor urged. "And drink some of this." He handed me the water glass.

"Kirsten. And I'm a Virgo." I took a sip of the ice cold water and shivered. "Couldn't you bring me room-temp water at least? You make a terrible nurse."

Conor frowned. "Okay. You seem coherent. You definitely seem like yourself. Are you sleepy at all?" Conor asked, crouching down in front of me.

I shook my head. "No."

"You didn't seem like you suffered a loss of consciousness. . . . Then again, you weren't exactly sure where you were when I picked you up." Conor gazed into my eyes. "But that happened the other night, too, when you were coming home after going sledding, and you didn't hit your head then. Or did you?"

"Do you have to insult me while I'm sitting here feeling a major headache coming on?" I grabbed my purse, which I'd left on the sofa earlier that day. "Which reminds me, I have some ibuprofen in here."

"Don't take anything yet. Hold on. I'm trying to remember all the things I should check," Conor said, tapping his fingers against my knees.

"Check?" I asked.

"For a concussion. Okay, a couple more things. Are you vomiting? No, you're not. Okay, I have to check your pupils," he said. "First I want to make sure they're both dilated the same amount—the same width. Look at me."

He was leaning close to me, staring into my eyes, when the front door flew open. We jumped back as Sean rushed in, panting and out of breath.

"I'm making sure she didn't hit her head too hard. Ruling out a concussion," Conor said.

"What are you, a doctor? You don't know anything about that!" Sean said.

"Yes, I do," Conor said. "Who do you think got a concussion once? Not you—me."

Was it me, or was this competition a little insane, when it came down to arguing over who had the most skull fractures?

"You're full of it." Sean sat on the sofa beside me and put his arm around my shoulders. "How are you feeling?" He gave me a little squeeze. "You okay?"

Conor pulled the fleece throw over my legs.

"You can go now," Sean said.

"I want to make sure she's okay," Conor said.

"I'll look after her," Sean said. He got up and followed Conor to the door. I could hear them arguing, but I was starting to get a headache, so I just leaned back against the pillows and relaxed. The door closed, and I assumed Conor was gone.

"How's it going?" Sean asked.

I wasn't sure if I was still seeing things. There was a hazy light. "Hey," I said.

"You okay? Really?"

"Yeah, well. I should probably borrow Brett's helmet next time I try to take Bear down to the rink."

"Ouch."

"But other than that, I'm fine."

"Good." He took off his hat and rubbed his head, making his hair do that cute static-y thing. "I kind of have some bad news for you, though. Something I forgot to tell you."

"What. You can't go skiing that weekend?" I sat up so quickly that I did actually feel dizzy for a moment or two.

"What weekend?"

"Sean!" I threw the fleece blanket toward him. "I told you a hundred times, Groundhog Day weekend—"

"I know, I know! Sorry. I just forgot for a second there."

"You did check to see if you can come. Right?"

He nodded, handing the blanket back to me. "But I have to tell you I'm not completely sure yet. Because Coach keeps changing our schedule around, and we might have this game scheduled with a college JV team that day, but hopefully not. Anyway, the bad news I had to tell you is that . . . I'm not going to see you anymore—"

"What?" How much bad news did he expect me to take in one sitting?

"This week," he finished the sentence. "I'm going away for four or five days, to North Dakota for a hockey camp thing and a tournament. We're leaving tomorrow, actually."

"Oh. Is that all?" I leaned back on the pillows with a contented sigh. He still wasn't completely sure about the Groundhog Getaway, but what was more important, really? The fact he was here with me now, or the fact I could bring him to meet all my friends?

Wait a second. That was a tough call.

Sean smiled and snuggled close to me on the sofa. "So I'll see you when I get back. It should be a couple days before the Snow Ball," he said.

"Speaking of which. What should I wear?" I asked.

"You know that habit you have of not wearing enough clothes or layers? Go with that." He grinned at me.

"Okay, but I'm not wearing the Snow White costume," I replied.

Chapter 14

$\mathcal{C}$onor had my double latte ready even before I claimed a table. He brought it over as I sat down, sliding the mug toward me.

"Thanks for making sure I got home okay the other day."

"Oh. No problem," he said.

I could tell that we both sort of flashed on that awkward moment when he was gazing into my eyes, and Sean walked into the house.

"See anything?" he asked, pointing to the mug.

"A very hot coffee with my name on it?" I asked. "Oh, you probably want your three dollars, don't you?"

"Plus tip, yeah." He smiled. "But that's not what I was talking about."

I looked around the bakery café, wondering if they'd made some change I hadn't noticed when I walked in. All I noticed were several new posters for Winter Carnival on the bulletin board.

"I made a pattern." Conor gestured toward the mug again.

"What?" I felt confused.

"A pattern. In the foam. It's . . . well, it's supposed to be a snowball. It kind of looks like a formless blob, now, doesn't it." He pulled over an empty chair from the next table and straddled it.

"Does that really look like a snowball to you?" I joked. "Well, snow, maybe. It is white." I lifted the coffee cup to my lips to take a sip.

"Thanks."

"Hey—part of the reason I came here is because we need to order a cake for Brett's birthday."

"Cool! Hold on a sec." Conor got up from the chair and went over to the counter. He came back carrying a small piece of paper.

"How old is he going to be?" Conor asked. "Four, right?"

"Right," I said.

"Vanilla? Chocolate?" he suggested. "No, wait. It's Brett. It has to be strawberry." He tapped his pen against the table. "We don't actually make a strawberry cake. How about a white cake with strawberry frosting?"

"That'd work," I said.

"What did Gretchen say?"

"She said get anything, but make sure it's not her favorite. She's been trying to lose weight. Her fave is chocolate, so this should be safe."

"What's your favorite?" Conor asked.

"Mine?" I laughed. "Chocolate, too. With chocolate frosting. No, wait—even better? Banana cake with chocolate icing—"

"Yeah, but have you ever had raspberry chocolate cake?" Conor said. "The baker here makes a killer torte like that."

"A killer torte," I repeated. "Hmm."

"Yeah, okay, maybe I've been working here too long. So, about this coffee thing," Conor said.

"What . . . coffee thing?" I wondered.

"The snowball. Have you heard about this Snow Ball party thing?" Conor asked.

Oh, no, I thought. He wasn't really going to do this, was he? "Is everything a thing?" I joked.

"Hey, I'm all about the *things*," he replied.

I laughed, hating to tell him something he wouldn't want to hear. Because it seemed like he was about to invite me to the party, though I couldn't understand why. Did he think Sean and I had a falling-out? Or had we had one . . . without Sean telling me? Was there something I didn't know?

"Remember that day at Buck Hill?" I said.

"Unfortunately," Conor mumbled. "I mean— not the hanging out with you part. The being on a float part."

"We weren't on a float, we were on a bed!" I said.

A few people sitting at the table beside us turned to look when I said that. Conor and I looked at each other and laughed.

"Same difference. So what were you saying?" Conor asked.

"Oh. Just that, yeah. Sean asked me to the Snow Ball then. I'm sorry, Conor."

"Oh, it's cool. You know, I just thought . . .

you're here. I'm here. The party is fun." He shrugged. "We could have fun together, snarking on the seven hockey players and their dates." He coughed. "Six hockey players. Whatever."

"Sorry." I shrugged.

"Yeah. Well, speed has never really been one of my strong suits. Actually I don't even have a suit, which is going to be a problem if I go to this thing, so maybe it's just as well."

We sat there in awkward silence for a minute. I willed Bear to bark at a police car siren, to race off with a heavy metal object, anything. Just get me out of this weird situation.

Finally Conor forced a smile. "Well, maybe I'll see you there if I get that suit thing together. In the meantime, I'd better get this cake order turned in." He stood up and shoved the chair back to its original table.

About twenty minutes later, I was about to go ask Conor for a coffee refill when he suddenly grabbed his coat and left the bakery. He didn't even say goodbye to me. I watched him walk down the block and then turn the corner.

"Where's he going?" I asked Paula when I

went up to the counter. She held out her hand, and I held out my mug.

"He went to the market. We're almost out of half-and-half and our delivery's not until later today," Paula said. "What did you *say* to him, anyway? You'd think he was dying."

"Not much," I said. "He asked me to go to this party, but I couldn't go with him because I'm going with his brother."

"Oh. *Oh*." Paula nodded. "No wonder he's acting like this. Do you know how much he and his brother compete? And do you know how long it's been since he liked anyone?"

Liked anyone? I thought. So Conor really did like me—he wasn't just inviting me to spite Sean? "How long?" I asked.

"I don't know, exactly," Paula said. "But I've known him a year and there's been no one. Absolutely no one."

"Oh," I said. I was surprised. Conor kind of sounded like me. He didn't go around dating just to date. He hadn't had tons of girlfriends, just like I hadn't had more than one boyfriend, and even he hardly counted.

So what was my situation now? I wondered.

Did I have a boyfriend, or just a date for the Snow Ball?

I went back to my table, sat at the computer, and emailed Jones. I wanted her advice, her take on things. I wanted to know what I should do. Instead I just asked her:

> JONES, are you coming down for
> Winter Carnival or not?

Before she could respond, Conor walked back into the bakery carrying three plastic bags, filled with cartons of milk and half-and-half.

I waited a minute to let him get settled, then walked over to the counter. "Want to go to Winter Carnival tomorrow?" I asked.

"What?"

"Do you want to go to Winter Carnival with me tomorrow? My friends were supposed to come down, but I don't know if they're going to."

He frowned.

Oh, no. I'd totally said the wrong thing. I'd blurted out this invitation without thinking it through. Of course he didn't want to go with me. I was seeing his brother; it was probably wrong for me to hang out with him.

"It's okay. You don't have to," I said quickly. "Never mind. It was just a . . . you know. An idea."

"No, it's not that I don't want to." Conor opened the fridge under the counter and started loading it with half-and-half. "I'm supposed to work at Zublansky's tomorrow afternoon, but maybe I can get someone to cover for me. I was just wondering who, and how much I'd have to bribe them."

"I'll pitch in a few bucks," I offered.

He seemed kind of taken aback by that. Too forward, I wondered? But we were just friends—what I was saying was exactly what I'd say to Jones.

"Brett would have to come, too," I said. "Is that okay?"

"Sure. No problem," Conor said. "Could you leave Bear at home though? I don't necessarily think we should let him knock down any other people trying to check out the carnival."

"I'll take Bear to the off-leash park so he can run as long as he wants. Then we can be gone for a while and he won't miss us," I said. "And I'll make sure Gretchen can handle us all being gone. What am I talking about? I'm sure she can. It's like her dream when Brett and I leave the house."

Conor laughed. "Really?"

"Oh, yeah," I said. "I don't know what she's going to do when I leave to go home, actually. She's gotten really used to having me around."

"Me too," Conor said. Then he cleared his throat loudly. "You're, you know, kind of blending in here. With the furniture."

"Thanks. I guess." I looked behind me at the tables and chairs. I didn't see any similarities, but whatever.

"Anyway, about Winter Carnival." Conor crumpled the now-empty plastic bags. "Normally I don't go to that kind of thing."

"You don't? Why not?" I asked. "I love Winter Carnival."

"Well, I'm not really into mini-donuts and pork chops on sticks." Conor made a face. "Ever since I ate too many one summer at the State Unfair."

I laughed. "That sounds like a radical political group."

"No, it's just what I call the 'big get-together,'" Conor said, making a reference to the ad campaign for the Minnesota State Fair. "I definitely haven't liked it since I lost in the pie-eating competition, actually. Though I do like the milk bar and the butter sculptures."

"Pie-eating? Don't tell me about it. And don't tell me about racing to eat any butter sculptures, either. But who did you lose to?" I asked.

"I don't know. Some guy from Roseville. Why?"

"Just wondering," I said. I'd figured that he must have lost to Sean, since it seemed like all they did was compete against each other, and gloat over who was better.

"You know something? You have a lot of emotional baggage when it comes to the State Fair. What, do you just have to leave the state every August, so you don't have flashbacks?" I teased him. "What's the clinical term for that? Post-traumatic fair disorder?"

"Yeah, well, *anyway*. I normally avoid these

kinds of organized-fun-slash-torture events, but Winter Carnival can be kind of fun. Sure. I'll go," he said.

"Great." I smiled at him.

Chapter 15

"Don't fall," Conor warned as I stepped out of the minivan. "It's really icy right here."

"And I have a history of falling. Is that what you're saying?" I opened the side door and unclipped Brett from his car seat. He looked a little drowsy, but I had no doubt he would perk up once he saw the crowds of people milling around downtown St. Paul.

Fortunately, we had a stroller with us, and it was one that Brett even liked.

"Just be careful." Conor tapped the ice with his boot. "They could use a little more sand here."

"That's right—I forgot I was traveling with Mr. Snow Removal," I teased him.

"Hey, did you or did you not whack your head

on the ice? Speaking of which, you feeling any after-effects?"

I shook my head. "No, but Gretchen made me go to the doctor with her yesterday just to make sure."

"And? What did the doctor say?"

"She said Gretchen's leg is healing. Slowly." I unfolded the stroller, helped Brett climb into it, then slipped the necessity bag into its bottom basket. "And then Gretchen and I went to the spa to get manicures and look at possible new hairstyles. She has this habit of trying to give me makeovers whenever she's stressed. Her coping mechanism is to try changing me."

Conor laughed. "You're not really going to cut your hair, though," he said. "Are you?"

"No." I blushed.

"Cool."

As we started walking out of the RiverCentre parking ramp, Conor pointed to the huge brick buildings around us. "That's the Science Museum, but you probably knew that. And here's the Xcel Energy Center, where the Minnesota Wild plays. The NHL team."

"Wouldn't it be cool if we could go to a

game?" I asked. "I mean, a bunch of us."

"Yeah. It's fun—I've been to a few," Conor said. "I used to think I could play hockey that well. Ha!"

"Maybe you can," I said. "Just because you got cut from the school team that doesn't mean you have to give up."

"Yeah. Or I could transfer to a school with a bad team," Conor said. "Not that I know of too many around here. Maybe I could transfer to somewhere in Hawaii." He laughed. "Anyway, the state high school hockey tournament is at the Xcel, too. Have you ever been?" he asked.

"Two years ago," I said. "Our school made it to the quarterfinals. Even that was a huge deal."

"Oh, yeah. That's nothing. When Sean was a sophomore he scored a hat trick. The place went wild." Conor rolled his eyes. "I was proud of him, but it was a little disgusting."

I decided to change the subject. "Is that like a miniature ice palace?" I pointed to a structure made of ice blocks in the park we were heading toward.

"That's not an ice palace. That looks more like an ice fishing shack," Conor commented.

As we got closer, we saw that it was intentional: The piece was titled "Ice Fishing Palace." Conor smiled. "Well, we were both right."

We walked around and checked out the other sculptures: a huge one of the State Capitol, an eagle, and a big wedge of Swiss cheese with holes carved into it, and tiny ice mice running on top of it. In the center of the park, a carver was working with a chainsaw on a plain large ice block, making a silhouette of a woman's face, who was modeling for him.

As we walked over to another plaza to look at the snow sculptures, Brett suddenly decided it was time for him to start playing hide and seek. He hopped out of the stroller and sprinted right past the chains protecting a giant sculpture of a lion. "Roarrrr!" he yelled as he ran toward it.

"Sorry," I said to the women working, as I scooped up Brett and retrieved him before he could do any major damage. He started crying right away, and nothing I could say made him feel better. I showed him the train made of snow, and the Santa Claus, and the dog. . . . Still, he kept crying.

"Hey, Brett. I have an idea," Conor said.

"Wh—wh—what," Brett sniffled.

"I heard there's a snowman-making contest here. Do you want to help me build a snowman?"

Brett wiped his eyes and looked up at Conor. "A snowman?"

Conor nodded. "A snowman. You and me. We'll win a ribbon, I promise."

"God, you're competitive," I commented. "Do you ever stop?"

"Everyone gets a ribbon just for trying," he said under his breath to me. "I used to do this when I was a kid. Okay? Come on, Brett." He took Brett's hand and they started skipping toward the area where giant mounds of fresh snow had been dumped, and small, very round stacked figures rose in the distance. "Let's build!"

"Told you we'd get a ribbon." Conor dangled the blue ribbon with a Winter Carnival button hanging from it in front of my face.

"You *bought* that," I said. Buttons were used to gain entrance to different carnival events;

they cost five bucks, and the design changed each year, so they made cool collectibles when the events were all over.

"Well, the button, yeah, I did buy that. But we earned the ribbon. Right, Brett?"

"We won, Aunt Kirsten!" Brett cried happily.

"Well, good for you. I'm very proud of you." I pulled Brett's hat down a little, because he was about to lose it. "Are you hungry? You want a snack?"

He nodded eagerly, so we headed over to a couple of ice blocks to sit down. While I was getting a handful of peanut butter crackers out of the "everything" bag, I noticed a bus pull up, and suddenly girl after girl after girl was stepping off the bus, each one wearing a little tiara—like my Snow White one!—and a sash bearing the name of a town or suburb. Miss Owatonna, Miss Robbinsdale, Miss Stillwater, Miss Congeniality. . . .

Where had they come from? What were they doing here? I knew the Winter Carnival crowned King Boreas and a Snow Queen every year, but this wasn't the same thing. They started checking out the giant star-shaped ice sculptures where Conor was standing.

"See this? I won this." He held the ribbon and button up in front of Miss Eden Prairie.

She laughed at him. "Yeah, whatever."

"Oh! Harsh." He put his hand over his heart. "You guys want me to take your picture?" he asked as the mob of girls circulated around the giant stars.

I took out my camera phone and started taking Conor's picture, as he posed with Miss Winona and the others.

"What can I say, I've always had a thing for princesses," he said as he walked over to me. "Ah, royalty."

I raised my eyebrow and glared at him.

"Kidding. Kidding!" he said. "I was doing my best imitation of Sean. He was junior prom king, you know."

"Ew. My sister was prom queen. Me, on the other hand, I've never actually worn a sash."

"I'll go borrow one for you," Conor offered.

"No! Don't!" I called as he headed back to the group of girls.

He stopped and turned around. "Why not?"

"Because. I—I don't know what size I take."

"Um, I don't think they come in sizes." He started talking to different girls, and pointing over at me and Brett. Most of them looked at him as if he were insane, but a couple of them seemed to be considering it. Finally he came jogging over to me carrying a white sash with blue letters that said: Miss Midwest. I stood up and Conor draped the sash over my head.

"Wow, I get to be the whole Midwest? I must have some sort of hidden talent," I said.

"Classical piano," the girl said with a smile as she walked over to me. She held out her hand. "I'm Christie."

"Kirsten," I said, being careful to shake her hand gently, given that she was a piano-playing virtuoso. "You sure it's okay if I wear this for a second?"

"You can take one picture," she said. "Then I have to get back to the bus—we're on a schedule. Also I think it's against policy, so be quick about it."

"Thanks!"

"And who are you?" Christie asked Brett, keeping him busy while Conor snapped a quick photo of me.

"You'll always be Miss Midwest to me," he said.

"Gee. Thanks," I said.

We drove from downtown St. Paul over to Como Park, for the Frosty Fingers kite fly.

"Why are we doing this again?" Conor said as we trudged across the snow to Lake Como, where kites danced in the air. The wind had begun to howl a little, and some freezing rain was falling.

Brett was riding on Conor's shoulders, and for that reason maybe the wind chill at that height was hitting him a little harder than usual. When I glanced up to check on him, I could have sworn his lips were turning blue.

Then I remembered the fruit-flavored snow-cone he'd insisted on having earlier. That was syrup stain on his mouth, not frostbite.

Still, I suggested we blow off the kite flying and head to the other side of Como Park, to visit the conservatory. We regrouped and headed indoors to look at plants and enjoy warm, humid air. Afterward, we took Brett over to the historic carousel, and I took pictures of him and

Conor going around on a wooden horse, making faces at me each time the carousel circled past.

All in all, it was a totally fun, totally exhausting afternoon.

"What next?" I asked as we walked away from the carousel, after I'd somehow managed to convince Brett that the Como Zoo was closed because it was too cold for the animals. It wasn't closed, but I was too cold, and technically I am an animal of some sort, so it wasn't a total lie.

Fifteen minutes later, Brett was sound asleep. We gently put him into his car seat and started the engine so the minivan would warm up.

We stood outside the car for a minute, and I felt Conor looking at me, out of the corner of my eye.

"What?" I asked as I turned to him.

"Oh, nothing. I was just thinking. You must be freezing." Conor moved closer to me, practically snuggling against my side.

All I could think was, *He's about to kiss me, this is a move, he's totally about to kiss me.*

Chapter 16

"So, let's see how all those pictures we took turned out," I said, backing away from Conor. "I can't wait to see them!"

"Oh. Okay." Conor shrugged.

I resisted the urge to ask him, *What were you thinking?*

Or maybe the better question was: What was I thinking? Because I'd had to drag myself away, because I was pretty sure that if he didn't kiss me, I would kiss him.

Maybe the cold was getting to us and our survival instincts were kicking in, I thought. Not that kissing has ever saved anyone from frostbite, but you never knew.

We leaned against the minivan and let it

shield us from the strong wind. I got out my camera phone and we started clicking through all the images we'd taken during the day, laughing at the goofy ones, deleting the embarrassingly bad ones. I decided to send one of me, Conor and Brett posing in front of the ice fishing palace to Jones.

A minute or two later, there was a little bell chime, and the icon for a text message popped up on my phone screen. Without thinking, I clicked on the button to open it.

You and Sean = cute! it said.

I smiled nervously at Conor. "Oops. Maybe I should use captions from now on."

That's not Sean, I typed back to her.

"She has a point, you know." Conor adjusted his gloves, pulling them up higher on his wrists.

"What?"

"You and I do look good together. Not that I care about superficial things like that, but it's true." He pointed to another photo. "I mean, you have to admit we make a cool couple."

A cool couple? What was he talking about? I flipped my phone closed. "Well, we should probably get going, don't you think? Brett's asleep, and it's getting even colder—"

"Okay, but first, can I ask you something?" Conor turned sideways and leaned against the minivan.

"That depends." I smiled at him. "What is it? Is it whether I'm going to use Jones's line in my project?"

"No. It's . . ." He peered into the minivan at Brett to check on him. "Why are you going out with Sean?"

I'm sorry, I thought. *But isn't that really, really personal? And also: I'm not really ready for this.* "Um . . . what do you mean?" I asked.

"Why are you going to the party with him, when you and I obviously have more in common, and have more fun together?" Conor finally turned away from the window to look at me. "Why don't you go with me instead?"

I didn't know what to say. He had a point.

Lately whenever I spent time with Conor, I noticed that we had more to talk about, that we never struggled for things to say.

"I'm really flattered," I said.

"Oh God. That's the kiss of death," Conor muttered. "Whenever someone says that, it means, I don't actually think of you that way."

"But I can't . . . I can't change things and go to the dance with you," I said.

"I don't get it. Why not?"

"Well, first of all, I'd have to break my date with Sean."

"He'd get over it. Believe me."

That wasn't exactly a compliment. "See, uh, we made a deal. Sort of." This was sounding pathetic; it wasn't about the fact we had a deal. It was that I was sort of stunned by what Conor just said. Maybe I *was* more interested in him than Sean. Only what was I supposed to do about it now?

"A deal?" Conor sounded suspicious.

"It's this big Groundhog Day weekend thing . . . with my friends—skiing and going to a cabin up north," I said. "They made me get a date, they insisted I bring someone. I mean, they only want me to be happy and everything—it's not like if I showed up alone, they wouldn't let me in the door or something." I laughed nervously. "So anyway, the day we went to Buck Hill, Sean asked me to the Snow Ball, and I said I'd go with him if he came on this long weekend trip with me—"

"Wait a second. You're going away with him for a whole weekend? Are you serious?" Conor asked.

I nodded.

"I mean . . . are you that serious about Sean? I didn't realize," Conor said.

"Really?" I asked.

"Well, yeah. If I knew about it, I wouldn't have been spending so much time with you."

What did he mean by that? Did he think it was bad manners? Was it? And why hadn't Sean told him that the two of us were going away? Was he planning to come, or wasn't he? Wouldn't he have had to ask permission from his parents, and wouldn't Conor know about that?

Anyway, was I serious about Sean, like Conor said? Not really, I had to admit. I liked him, but did I see us going out, long-term? I hadn't gotten that far yet.

"No—see . . . we are going away for the weekend, but it's not . . . like that. I mean, it is like that, but it's only a little trip," I said.

Conor shook his head. He looked a little disgusted by me at that moment. "No, you can't have it both ways. You're either with him or you're not. And since you're going out with him, and then going away for the weekend, I'm thinking you're with him. I don't know why you'd *want* to be, but that's your problem." He stepped away from the minivan. "Look, can we go now?"

"Yeah, okay." I started to walk around to the driver's door. But instead of getting into the car, Conor followed me around it.

"So what was the plan, exactly?" he said as I opened the door. "You needed a guy for the weekend? Were you comparing us or something?"

"Conor. Please," I said. "I didn't have a—a plan. Things just happened."

He raised one eyebrow. "Things don't just happen," he said.

"But they did!" I protested. "Sean and I just sort of . . . we kept running into each other. And he seemed to like me, and you . . . you didn't. I mean, you mocked me half the time, and ignored me the other half."

"I don't know what you're talking about," Conor said. "I've been nice to you since day one, since the day you got here."

I had to shake my head at that. "Wait a second. Wait a second," I sputtered. "Are you talking about *you*? Nice to me since day one? Have you listened to yourself lately?"

"What," Conor said. "What are you talking about, I'm nice."

"Yeah, *now* you are. Maybe. But how about the time you called me stupid? No, wait, that was like five times. Maybe if you had been nice to me, like you claim, I wouldn't even have looked at Sean."

"Sure you would have," Conor scoffed. "Every girl does."

"Okay. Maybe I *would* have looked." He had a point there. "But I definitely didn't sense any interest coming from you."

"Wh—what? Are you serious? How about

when I made your coffee all those times? How about when I always made sure I bagged your groceries?"

I laughed. "But those are your *jobs*!" I pointed out.

He seemed a little stunned by that news. "Well, how about when I went along sledding that night, and to the mattress race to make sure you were safe with those guys?"

"You didn't need to come along just to protect me. I can take care of myself!" I said.

"Fine. Then do it," he said. "And have a really great time spending the weekend with Sean. I don't know how you *could*, but—"

"Don't be like that," I said. "Okay?"

"Sorry. Apparently I am like that," Conor said.

We stood there for a second, glaring at each other. "Look. Let's go. I need to get Brett home, and you probably have to work somewhere—"

"I'll get home by myself. Thanks but no thanks." He started to walk away, across the parking lot.

"Conor!" I called after him. "Come on, you live practically next door. Don't be ridiculous."

"Sorry, that's just me being me," he said as he threw up his hands and did his best helpless look.

I sighed. "Come on, *please*. I don't know the way."

"No kidding," he muttered. "Don't you think you should learn your way around if you're going to be here for a few months?"

"I don't know how long I'm going to be here," I said. "Maybe not that long."

"Fine. Get a map then," Conor said.

"Conor. I promise, it's the last favor I'll ever ask you. Could you *please* show me the way?" I asked.

"All right. Whatever." He reluctantly trudged back to the minivan and climbed into the passenger seat.

The whole way home, all Conor said to me was, "Right here. Go left. Left. Right."

Fortunately for Brett, he slept right through it.

I couldn't tell Conor that in many ways, I actually liked him more than Sean. That I liked the way that lately (at least until just now in the parking lot) he always looked after me, made sure I was doing okay. That he'd come off a little rude and standoffish at first, but that he'd grown on me. That I'd rushed into asking Sean and made a huge error in judgment because of my dumb timeline, because I needed to prove to everyone—including myself—that I could get a great guy.

Which was so superficial, when you got right down to it, that it could almost make me sick. Or else make me Gretchen. Here I was, set up to attend the big dance with Mr. Popular. The Gretchen in me was thrilled; the Kirsten in me would maybe rather take a rain check.

When we got home, I pulled over in front of Conor's house. He jumped out and slammed the door behind him. "Yeah, it was nice hanging out with you, too!" I called after him as he ran up the walk to his front door.

Fortunately, the windows were closed so he couldn't hear me.

When I carried the still-sleeping Brett into the house and put him in his crib, Gretchen was nowhere to be found. That was strange.

No more strange than what had just happened with Conor, but still strange.

I was tempted to call my friends right away

and ask them what to do, but I had a feeling this was something I'd have to sort out for myself.

That night, I awoke with a start. Something was hitting my bedroom window. At first I thought it was probably sleet, from the sound of it. But after being awake for a minute, I realized it wasn't sleet—it was rocks. Or pebbles.

Conor! I thought instantly. Maybe it was Conor coming to apologize.

Wait. Coming in the middle of the night didn't seem like Conor's style, exactly. Besides, he did sort of hate me right now. I didn't see him as the kind of person who would smooth things over that quickly; he seemed like the type to hold a grudge for eternity.

I pulled a sweater on over my PJs and slid my feet into my furry boots, then I went to the front door. I peered out the little window on the door to make sure I knew who was throwing pebbles at the window.

Yup. I knew him, all right.

"Hey," I said, opening the door.

"We just got back!" Sean wrapped his arms

around my waist and gave me a big hug.

"It's nice to see you," I said.

"You, too. I really missed you," he said, giving my waist an extra squeeze. And then a little pinch, as he came into the house.

"Mmm," I said. Had I missed him? I hadn't really thought about him much. That wasn't a good sign, was it? He was acting like he was really excited to see me. Coming over in the middle of the night?

"Love those PJs," he said.

"Thanks," I said.

"Here, I got you a little gift." He handed me a small white box, which I was almost afraid to open. Not that I don't like presents, but it seemed like an odd time to be giving me one. Maybe that was why he'd come over in the middle of the night?

I opened the box. Inside was a strange-looking food product. "What is . . ." I picked up a little slip of paper from the candy company that explained things. "Chocolate-covered potato chips. Huh."

"Yeah, aren't they cool?" Sean asked.

I put one in my mouth and crunched it.

"Surprisingly yummy," I said.

I held the open box out to him, but he shook his head. "No thanks, I ate a box on the bus ride home."

I laughed. "Well, thanks for these. That's so sweet of you. How was Fargo?"

"We had a great time. Played like two games a day, plus we met with coaching scouts from different colleges. I think I really impressed them."

"That's cool."

"What have you been up to?" Sean asked.

Spending time with your brother. And completely alienating him, I thought.

"Not much," I said. "The time went by kind of quickly, actually."

"Oh yeah? That's good."

And then we awkwardly looked at each other for a few seconds. Sometimes I wondered what he was doing with me, when we had these lulls in conversation and not that much to talk about. Then again, what was I doing with him? Half the reason I was dating him was to win some stupid challenge with my friends, and myself, to not go the entire senior year without a date. To have a romantic weekend just because.

"So do you want to hang out by the fire for a while? Maybe have some hot chocolate?" Sean asked.

"With our chocolate chips?" I wrinkled my nose. "I don't know. I don't actually want any hot chocolate. I don't think."

"No?" He seemed disappointed.

I shook my head. "No."

"What's wrong?" Sean asked.

"I . . . I don't know. Just sleepy, I guess." I stretched my arms over my head and yawned, for effect.

"Okay, I'll leave you alone." He smiled and gave me a little kiss on the cheek. "Snow Ball in two days, are you ready?"

"Not yet." I pictured the latte Conor had made, with the special foamed milk snowball on top. "But I will be," I said with a faint smile. "Now would you let me go back to sleep?"

"Okay, okay. See you later!" Sean leaned down to kiss me goodnight, but I turned at the last second so that he kissed my cheek instead.

Chapter 17

"You what?"

"I asked Conor to deliver Brett's birthday cake today. I figured we'd be too busy blowing up balloons and so forth."

"You didn't."

"I did," Gretchen said.

"You asked Conor to deliver it here?" I nearly shrieked. "Gretchen! I could kill you right now."

"Why?" she asked.

That's when I remembered that she didn't know about the whole Conor situation. All she knew was that I was going to the Snow Ball with Sean, and she was beside herself with excitement about that.

Wait until I told her we were going away for the weekend together. I hadn't told her yet, because I was dreading her reaction. She knew I had plans to go on a trip with my friends that weekend, because I'd arranged that as soon as I got to her house.

"Why are you going to kill me?" she asked. "I was trying to do you a favor by not asking you to go pick up the cake. I figured you'd be busy enough getting ready for tomorrow night."

"Well!" I cleared my throat. "That's just it. I mean, first of all, you're taking over this whole thing and acting like it's your party, not mine."

Gretchen had been jumping for joy—almost literally, almost bouncing off her crutches—ever since I told her that Sean had invited me to the Snow Ball. She'd read about the party in the newspaper's society sightings page and had been curious about it ever since.

"I knew he'd ask you. This is so perfect! This is great!" she kept crying when I finally told her about it.

I had to tell her to back off. "Gretchen! I'm not like your protégé. You're living through me or something weird like that."

"Can't I be excited for my little sister?" She looked very hurt.

"I'm sorry," I said, "but I'm a little stressed out about all this."

So today, we'd spent the morning at a few malls, searching for the perfect dress for me. Finally we'd found something we both liked: it was strapless, a cool gold color, very classic and wintry looking. And according to Gretchen and the saleswoman (basically clones of each other), it looked great with my hair and slightly golden skin.

Whatever.

Gretchen had sprung for the gown, to thank me for everything I'd done to help her out over the past few weeks. But of course she'd also sprung for new shoes to match it, and a wispy scarf to wear over my shoulders, and some new gold nail polish that would match it.

And of course, a gown for herself. She'd lost ten pounds and was pretty excited about it, not to mention the fact she couldn't go shopping without buying something for herself.

"Come on, forget about Brett's silly birthday cake. Let's talk about the party some more. Right now I'm going to teach you how to waltz," she announced.

"What?" I cried. "I'm not going to have to waltz!"

"Yes, you are," she said.

"How would you know, you've never gone to this thing," I snapped. "Sorry. I'm just feeling a little, um, stressed. I won't know anyone else there, you know?"

"Don't worry about it. But that's why you should learn to dance, because it never hurts to be ready for any situation. Emily Post, page 341."

"Seriously?" I asked.

"Well, it's in there *somewhere*." Gretchen put on a CD of classical music. Then she hopped over to me, swinging on one crutch. "Come on, take my hands," she said.

"Gretchen, they're going to have a band. Like, a band that we'd all actually *want* to dance to," I told her. "Music from the twenty-first century. I'm not waltzing with my sister, on crutches no less."

"Do you want to look silly, or don't you?" she asked.

"Hello? Look at us right now," I said, laughing.

"Come on. Follow my lead," she urged. "One-two-three, one-two-three . . ."

Suddenly Gretchen's eyes widened.

"What? Did I step on your toe?" I said. "Did I hurt your broken leg? Oh no."

She shook her head, still staring over my shoulder.

I turned around and saw Conor standing in the doorway, large white bakery box in hand. "Sorry. I knocked. But no one answered, so . . ."

"It's okay!" I said. "Gretchen was, uh, imparting some of her dancing wisdom."

"Where should I put this?" He skillfully closed the door behind him with his foot.

"In the kitchen," I said. "Come on, I'll, uh, help you."

"It's all right, I've got it," he said as I trailed him down the hall to the kitchen.

I didn't care if he had it, or not, I wanted to talk to him for a second. "So. How have you been?" I asked.

"Busy," he said. "You know." He carefully set the cake box on the counter, sliding it toward the wall so it couldn't be knocked off by a small child or a dog. Or a very klutzy eighteen-year-old named Kirsten.

"Can I look at it?" I asked.

"It's nothing special." He shrugged. "Kids' birthday cakes, you put a big number on them, decorate a little . . ."

"Did you do the decorating?" I asked.

He nodded. "Check it out after I leave," he said.

"Why—"

I heard Brett's shrieking before I heard his footsteps thundering down the stairs. He was chasing Bear. And my new golden dress was draped over Bear's back, and my scarf was wrapped around his neck tightly, like a fancy collar.

Brett, of course, was wearing one of my new shoes.

"Connnnnnoooorrrrr!" he screamed, right before he slammed into Conor's legs.

"Hey, buddy. How's it going?" Conor asked.

"Let's make a snowman!" Brett cried.

"I can't today. I don't have time. Sorry," Conor said.

"Please?" Brett begged.

"Brett, I have to get back to work," Conor

said. "Anyway, aren't all your friends coming over soon? For your birthday party? That's why I brought the cake."

Bear was still racing around with my gown on his back. Gretchen was hopping around after him on her good leg, trying to pull it off with one of her crutches.

"Bear. *Bear*," I said. "Come here. *Bear!*"

Conor grabbed Bear's collar on his way back down the hall. He got Bear to stand still, and removed the dress and scarf. He held them out to me. "Yours?"

"Uh, yeah. Thanks." I was standing there, doing nothing, completely stupefied.

"Sure. Hope it's still wearable. Well, good luck with the dancing. Rock on." He tipped his baseball cap to me and Gretchen, and went out the door.

"How embarrassing," I said as I peeked out the window to watch him drive off in the bakery's delivery van.

"Who cares? It's only Conor."

Only Conor.

I walked back into the kitchen and went over to investigate the birthday cake. We hadn't had cake in the house since I got here. If Brett's friends didn't show up on time, there would be a piece missing.

I opened the box. To my surprise, inside were two boxes: one large, and one small. I opened the large one first. It was a large layer cake with strawberry frosting and a snowman saying, "Happy Birthday, Brett!" and a giant number 4. It was perfectly decorated.

Then I opened the small box. Inside was a chocolate cupcake, with chocolate icing, and chocolate sprinkles on top. And a note that said:

> Here's your favorite, and Brett's favorite.
> See you at the party tomorrow night?
> —Conor

I smiled and felt this incredibly happy glow come to my face. He didn't hate me anymore. He was going to the Snow Ball, without me, but he was still going. So I'd know someone else— I'd have a friend there.

Or maybe more than a friend.

I quickly grabbed the little box and took it

upstairs to my room without showing Brett and Gretchen, where I could gaze at—and eat—the cupcake later, while I reread Conor's note a few more times.

"How does the cake look?" Gretchen asked when I walked back down into the living room. She was perched on the sofa, watching a video of her wedding.

"The cake looks . . . wonderful," I said. Especially the little cupcake in my favorite flavor.

As I sat down beside her on the sofa, I wondered what to do next. Should I cancel my date with Sean? Probably. But it was so last minute— that seemed mean, even if Conor had assured me that Sean would get over it.

I wasn't sure what to do. I couldn't talk it over with my sister. If I broke the date with Sean, nobody would be more upset about it than Gretchen. But it wasn't as if the shoes and the dress would go to waste . . . though the waltz lessons definitely would.

So I'd go to the dance with Sean. I'd have as nice a time as I could, but at some point during the night, I'd have to tell him that things had changed. That we wouldn't be going away for the weekend after all, because, as Conor pointed out, I couldn't have it both ways. I wasn't sure how to tell him that I might be falling for his brother. That wouldn't go over well. But I wouldn't be fake about things, either.

"Look at you." She pointed to me and Jones on the TV screen. We were jumping around the dance floor, doing the mashed potato, pumping our arms up and down. "All I ask is, tomorrow night?"

"Yeah?" I asked.

"You dance a little better than you did at my wedding."

We both laughed, and then Gretchen reached for a tissue, because she was starting to cry. "God. I haven't been able to look at this video in a long time. It makes me sad—but it's sort of fun, too."

I'd hardly ever seen her cry. It was strange. She was usually so tough, acting like she didn't care.

"I know you're in love with Sean and everything, but promise me you won't get married until you're older," Gretchen said.

"Oh, don't worry," I told her, dropping onto the sofa beside her. "I'm not getting married anytime soon."

And another thing, I could have added. *I'm not in love with Sean.*

Chapter 18

$\mathcal{I}$'d forgotten to ask Sean how we would get over to St. Paul for the Snow Ball. I could take the minivan, though I didn't really want to drive. I wondered if Conor was going to drive the three of us again, but that would be beyond awkward. Besides, it was hard to imagine the three of us crammed into the pickup in our dressy clothes.

My hair was blown and brushed out straight, falling on my shoulders. Gretchen had helped me put some small sprinkles of ice-like glitter in my hair and on my bare shoulders. She'd also done my makeup, again, which she was getting pretty good at doing.

I shifted by the doorway in my high heels,

and glanced at my watch. It was almost eight-fifteen, and Sean had said he'd pick me up at eight.

The night wasn't exactly off to the best possible start, but oh well. "Being fashionably late—that's something Emily Post recommends, right?" I asked Gretchen as I came back from the front hallway, where I'd been pacing.

"I don't know. But I think anything over ten minutes is rude." She frowned, then reached for the telephone. "I think I'll call over there, see what happened to him—"

"No. Don't!" I cried. "I mean, if anyone should call, it's me, but I'm giving him five more minutes."

"I don't approve," Gretchen said. "For the record. He should be here on time."

I walked back over and peered out the window. A long, black station wagon was pulling up at the curb. It wasn't a limo, but it was close. "Hey! That might be him," I said. *Don't tell me he rented a car for this*, I thought.

Gretchen limped over to me and gave my

makeup a final check. "You're going to be cold," she said. "Take this." She reached into the closet and pulled out her long, maroon down coat— the one that looked like a sleeping bag.

"Thanks, Mom, but I'll just take this instead." I didn't have a long coat with me, so I just put my puffy jacket over my shoulders. I didn't plan to wear it, much.

"That doesn't go with your dress!" she protested.

"Well, neither does that." I pointed to her coat.

"You're impossible. You don't wear a short jacket with a gown," she said.

"It's not a gown. It's a dress." Gretchen rolled her eyes when I said that. "And I'll just carry it, if you're so concerned." I balled up the jacket under one arm, and held my miniature purse with the other.

"You look silly," Gretchen said. "But cute."

"Thank you." I bowed.

I looked out the window at the car idling by the curb. Was Sean going to come in, or did I have to run out there myself?

But there he was, coming up the walk. I took

a deep breath and braced myself. Tonight wasn't going to be easy. At least not at the beginning. First I had to tell Sean that I'd fallen for his brother. Then I had to tell Conor that I wanted to be with him.

Very possibly, I should have done all this before right now.

Gretchen opened the door, and I stood behind her, feeling like it was too eager to be caught looking out the window for your date.

"Wow," Sean said as I stepped out from behind Gretchen. "You look gorgeous."

I smiled at Sean, who was standing in the open doorway, a bit stunned. "Thanks," I said. "You look pretty good yourself."

Sean was wearing a dark blue suit, and he looked a little like Ashton Kutcher. In other words, very, very good.

"Picture time. Picture time!" Gretchen cried.

I could have killed her. Literally. "You are so like Mom. *So* like her," I said.

"Don't say that. Say cheese," she replied.

Sean and I posed in the doorway, then we posed by the fireplace, then we posed with Brett.

Finally we convinced her that we really did

have to get going. I gave Brett a good-night kiss, arranged the little scarf on my shoulders, and Sean took my hand and guided me over the doorstep and down the front walk.

I walked around to the other side of the car with Sean, and saw a camera flash go off on the front walk.

"Gretchen. Do you really need a shot of us getting into the car?" I asked.

"Yes. Now be quiet and smile and wave."

I doubted that she caught my smile, because as soon as Sean opened the car door, I saw who was in the car: five other people, including what's-her-name from the lake. I think I would have rather gone in the old pickup, rust and Conor and all.

Sean and I slid into the front seat next to one of the seven hockey players, Duke, who was driving the car. The other four people were crowded into the backseat. Sean introduced me to everyone, and although I didn't catch everyone's names or figure out who had come with whom, I did get her name again: Melissa. She was wearing a sexy, white strapless dress, and she had olive brown skin and looked amazing, a shoo-in contestant for the upcoming "America's Next Top Model" season.

The fact that she was there didn't bother me the way it would have a few weeks ago, though it did seem a little tactless on Sean's part for us to all ride in the same car.

Me? I stuffed my down jacket at my feet and then sat back and tried to relax. We drove past Sean's house and I looked to see whether Conor's truck was parked outside. It was. My heart sank. Wasn't he going to the party?

"We should go out to eat first," Sean said.

"Aren't they having food at the party?" I asked.

"Yeah, but I'm starving," Sean said. "Come on, it'll be hilarious. We'll go somewhere cheap, and sit there in our suits."

"We're late, though. Let's just get there," Melissa said.

I turned around and gave her a half-smile. "I agree."

"Okay. You guys are probably right," Sean said. "I still think it'd be fun."

He reached over and turned up the car stereo's volume, and the music was sort of blaring. *This wasn't really me,* I thought. Also, the music was so loud that I couldn't talk to Sean then, the way I wanted to. I hadn't realized we were going to the party in a group.

The song stopped just as I was saying, "I need to talk to you!" in a loud voice.

"Uh oh, sounds serious," his friend Philip said.

"You're in trouble, dude," Duke added.

Everyone started laughing and pushing Sean's shoulders from the back seat and flicking the top of his head.

"Uh, later. At the party. That would be fine," I said, smiling at him.

He rested his hand on my leg. "No problem." Then the next song started to play, and we went screaming down the highway on-ramp at top speed.

The house was breathtakingly beautiful, with white lights strung across the arched portico. A gigantic white wreath hung on the front door, and a snowman held a sign that said "Enter here—Valet parking" in fancy script. We turned over the car to the valet and headed for the entrance, me still clutching my down jacket, Melissa still looking fantastic. I thought she might be there with Philip, but I couldn't tell. We were all sort of traveling as a pack.

There was a guest list that the doorman checked our names against, then all the girls were each handed a white rose. In the front entryway, which was as big as our entire house at home, there was a large ice sculpture of a king and queen, representing the Winter Carnival royalty. This was without question the fanciest, most elegant party I'd ever attended.

"What do Kevin's parents do for a living, exactly?" I asked Sean as I gazed around the luxurious mansion, like a little kid seeing Disney World for the first time.

"I have no idea," he said.

"Well, whatever it is, they should keep doing it," I said, and we both laughed.

The gigantic room where the party was being held was more like a ballroom than a living room. The lights were set low, and the setting was very romantic, if crowded. There was a cart in the corner, serving Sno-Cones; caterers circled with trays of fancy, homemade versions of Hostess Sno-Balls and glasses of ice water and punch—and fake snow was sprinkled here and there, on top of small, potted pine trees, on skis that were hung on the wall, beside two pairs of old-fashioned skates. Winter Carnival buttons were hanging from silver ribbons dangling from the ceiling, along with silver icicles.

"Wow," I said as we walked around the room, looking at everything and everyone. "This is so cool."

"Yeah," Sean said, nodding. "It was like this last year, too."

"How many people do you think are here?" I asked.

"About a hundred?" Sean guessed.

"At least," I said. "More like two hundred, maybe."

We stood there people-watching for a minute or two. It was sort of weird that we didn't have anything much to talk about.

"Good band," I commented.

"Yeah." Sean nodded.

We were both still standing there surveying

the scene, and the crowd. It was like we barely knew each other, we had so little to talk about.

I had to tell him that I'd changed my mind, that I didn't think we should go away for the weekend after all. Why was this so hard? I didn't think he'd be crushed, exactly, but it was something I'd never had to do before.

"You want to dance?" Sean asked as a new song started.

"Sure," I said.

I'd left my jacket at the coat check, and I set my tiny purse on a table, along with the white rose. For some reason this seemed like a crowd you could trust not to take your stuff.

We moved to the center of the dance floor, where about fifty other people were dancing. The band was playing covers of popular songs. Sean and I looked at each other a couple of times as we danced. Suddenly, out of nowhere, all of his friends descended onto the dance floor, surrounding us. It was actually kind of fun, except for the way Melissa kept trying to get close to Sean and bump his hips with hers.

After a couple of songs I decided to take a little break, so I moved off the dance floor. I walked around for a bit to check out the rest of the house, and as I was going past the front entryway, suddenly I saw Conor walk into the house.

The most surprising thing wasn't that he was wearing a cool, retro suit, with a skinny tie, and suede sneakers. It wasn't that he didn't see me right off.

It was that he had walked in with a girl on his arm. A petite, dark-haired girl with light brown skin and a very cool black-and-white wool checkered coat.

I couldn't believe it. What was he doing with a date? Then again, why shouldn't he be allowed to bring someone? Just because we'd hung out together and had a good time, that didn't mean he was banned from seeing someone else.

I kept sneaking glances at them as they checked her coat, and walked into the big room. Every time I did, they were laughing.

I walked back over to Sean, who was hanging out by the Sno-Cone cart with his friends and the other girls. He didn't even seem to notice that I was back, or that I'd been gone.

"So I just saw Conor," I said, sidling up beside Sean.

"Oh, yeah? You want a cone?" Sean asked.

I shook my head. "No thanks. I'm holding out for a snowball," I said. "So, uh. Conor. He has a date for tonight?"

"Yeah. Guess so." Sean nodded.

"Really," I muttered.

A minute later, Conor and the girl he'd come in with walked past us and gave us a small wave. I waved back, my arm completely lifeless. His date gave me a friendly smile.

Yeah, I'd be happy, too, I thought, as I listened to Sean and his friends go on and on about how great the season was going to be, and whether they'd make it to the tournament, and where they wanted to play college hockey. . . . *If I were with Conor.*

About half an hour later, after dancing to a few more songs and making some more small talk, I was sitting on a window seat, looking out at the snow that had begun to fall, and wondering how long I'd have to stay. Because we had come to the party with other people, I'd have to wait for them to want to leave. It didn't look as if I was going to get a chance to actually talk to Sean about things, and it didn't seem like I would see Conor much, either. The night wasn't exactly going my way, and I wasn't sure what to do about it.

A waiter walked past with a tray of the round snowball-shaped cakes, and I jumped up, nearly knocking him down. "Oh. Excuse me," I said.

"No problem," he replied.

"I just kind of wanted one of those," I said, feeling my face turn red.

He held the tray out to me and I lifted up one of the snowball cakes on a napkin. "Enjoy."

"Thanks." I took a bite of the coconut-covered cake, wondering why they'd serve something that was so difficult to eat without making a mess. There must be some etiquette about how to eat something this crumbly at a party. But if there was, I didn't know it. No doubt Gretchen would.

I was taking another very delicate bite when suddenly Conor was standing beside me.

"Wouldn't these be great for a snowball fight?" he asked.

I was so surprised to see him that I nearly choked on a coconut flake that went down the wrong way.

"I could totally see this place breaking into mayhem," Conor added.

I brushed my mouth with a napkin. "Food fight, you mean?"

"Yeah." Conor grinned. "Should we do it?"

"No," I said, looking around at everyone, all dressed up. "I don't think we'd be very popular."

"Do we care? Anyway, you're leaving soon, and nobody here really knows who you are anyway." He nudged me with his elbow. "Do it. Show 'em that pitching arm."

I didn't appreciate how close he was standing to me. It was really hard to have finally realized how I felt about him, and then see him walk in with someone else.

"It's not a pitching arm," I said, trying to move away a little. "First base, remember?"

Conor put his fingers around my arm, completely encircling it. "Definitely not a pitcher's arm. A little too skinny for that."

"Not skinny," I said, brushing at a crumb on my wrist. "Toned."

"Right. Toned." He grinned. "You're all about the toned. Or is it tonedness?"

"I think it's tone-ocity," I said. I finished the snowball and dabbed at my mouth.

"Tenacity, maybe. Look out, you missed a couple." Conor reached out and brushed a coconut flake off my mouth. He was standing really close to me.

I thought, *No fair*. No fair doing that to me. Didn't you come with someone else?

But for that matter, didn't I?

"Thanks," I said. I flagged down the server who was passing us and managed to get a glass of punch. Conor took one, as well.

I felt like I should make a toast. It wasn't New Year's Eve, but this party felt as if we'd all start singing "Auld Lang Syne" at the drop of a hat. Or a glass of punch.

"Well, cheers," I said as I tapped my glass against Conor's.

"What are we toasting?" he asked.

I adjusted the wrap on my shoulders, which

had slipped a little. "To spring?"

He laughed. "Why would you want spring?"

"I don't know." I gazed around the room, looking for Sean. I couldn't believe we'd come together; I hadn't seen him in at least twenty minutes. I wondered if it was the same for Conor and his date. "Maybe I've been here long enough," I said.

"I disagree," Conor said. "Respectfully and all, but still."

"Respectfully? That's not like you." I looked over at him and smiled.

"Well, on second thought, maybe you *have* been here long enough," Conor said, frowning.

I was about to ask him what he meant by that when two things happened. One, Sean appeared at my side, sliding his arm around my waist. Two, about three girls came over and said, "Hey Conor, want to dance? Come on. You're dancing."

"Sounds great," Conor said loudly as they pulled him out onto the dance floor.

"Where have you been?" Sean asked.

"Uh . . . right here?" I said as I watched Conor and the girls laughing and dancing together and my stomach did somersaults. "What about you?"

"I've been here the whole time," Sean said. "Well, some of the guys went outside for a while. And then Kevin was showing us around the place."

It's called a date, I thought, irritated. *Look into it!* Didn't he realize that I would know nobody here, and therefore he should look after me?

Then again, had I really missed him? Would I have been any happier if we'd spent the whole night standing side by side and not talking? At least this way one of us was having a good time.

"Anyway," Sean said, "do you want to dance?"

"Not really, thanks," I said.

"Come on, Kirsten. You have to," Sean said. "We've hardly danced together at all."

And whose fault is that? I thought. "Okay, sure. Let's dance."

As soon as we got out onto the dance floor, though, someone in the band decided it would be funny to play a slow ballad. So I awkwardly put my hands on Sean's shoulders, and we started moving slowly around the dance floor. I wouldn't call it dancing, exactly. Gretchen would go berserk if she could see this, I thought with a smile. All my waltzing practice gone to waste.

As we turned around, I saw Conor dancing with someone else—not the girl he came with, and not the three girls who'd pulled him onto the dance floor, but still another. What was it about these brothers? Conor was just as bad as Sean. They were chick magnets! And I for one didn't want to end up on the family refrigerator.

"So, Sean," I began. "You know the weekend we're going away together? That ski trip, up north?"

"Which weekend was that again?" he asked.

We circled again, and I exchanged glances with Conor. "It's next weekend," I said.

"Oh. Sorry," Sean said. "I kind of forgot."

"No, don't be sorry—it's okay. It doesn't matter if you remember. I—we're not going," I said.

"We're not? Oh. Well, cool." He waited a second and then said, "Why not?"

I hadn't thought this through very well yet. Should I tell him the truth, or lie? He might not be my idea of the perfect guy anymore, but he'd been pretty nice to me since I got here. He should at least know how I felt.

"Well, see—"

"Excuse me. May I cut in?" Melissa tapped Sean on the shoulder.

"By all means." I smiled at her. "Go right ahead."

Okay, part one of the night accomplished. I'd told Sean about the weekend and he wasn't completely heartbroken. Maybe I should be depressed about that, but I wasn't going to bother. He'd never really been able to commit to the idea of going, anyway, and he was obviously happiest around all his friends and potential girl-friends. Maybe he wasn't ready for just one girl yet—and if he was, it wasn't me, because I wasn't the girl for him, anymore than he was the guy for me. I felt badly about it, but I guess that sometimes you have to spend a lot of time with someone to find that out.

Now, for part two: Find Conor and talk to him and tell him he was right. That I couldn't spend all the time in the world with both of them. That I had to choose. That you didn't hang around a ton with one guy, but go away for the weekend with someone else (much less his younger brother).

I didn't see Conor on the dance floor, but it was pretty crowded, so I waited a minute or two until the song was over. Sean and Melissa were dancing, and they looked sort of cute because he was so tall and she was so short.

When the song ended, I looked around for Conor again. Nope.

I walked around the outside of the room, past the Sno-Cone cart and all the chairs, and the clumps of people talking and laughing. I went out into the entryway, wondering if he'd left. Then I headed down the hallway toward the bathrooms, thinking I might as well fix my hair and redo my lipstick before I made my big confession. (Living with Gretchen for a month was definitely having an effect on me.)

On the way down the hall, I stopped to peek into another large room. It was a den, with tall bookshelves, dim green lights, and—

Conor.

Conor was in there talking to the girl he'd come with, and they were leaning against the desk, deep in what must be a very private conversation. Their heads couldn't have been more than two inches apart. I was trying to decide just how bad it was when Conor turned in my direction; he must have sensed someone in the doorway.

I immediately held my tiny purse in front of my face, as if that would shield me. Then I raced back down the hallway for the front door. I grabbed my jacket from the coat check girl, threw a five-dollar bill at her for the fast service, and raced for the front door.

Unfortunately the ice sculptures in the entry had started to melt, because they were positioned right under a bright chandelier, and there was water on the hardwood floor.

So I wiped out and fell down in the middle of my dramatic exit.

As I've said maybe a few times before? Cursed.

A few people rushed over to see if I was all right, but I jumped up and hurried out the door.

Chapter 19

Why did it have to snow tonight? I was thinking as I stomped down Summit Avenue in the slush, my puffy coat over my shoulders, my dress slightly torn where I'd slipped and caught it on my shoe.

I wasn't wearing the right shoes in which to stalk off angrily. The shoes had these little pointed toes and these little spiky heels. I was getting snow on my feet and ankles, because not everyone had gotten around to shoveling yet—why would they? It was still snowing. I needed snow boots, not pretty, delicate party shoes.

Shoveling. Why did I even have to think of shoveling, which made me think of Conor, and that day I ran out and nearly tackled him with my hug.

Well, so much for Groundhog Getaway. That wasn't going to happen. And neither was anything with me and Conor.

Why had I even come? I didn't do well with fancy parties. Exhibit A: junior prom, where I thought I had a date but it turned out he liked someone else.

Exhibit B: Snow Ball. Where I also thought I had a date, and I did, but I didn't like him, and the guy I did like showed up with another date.

And they were brothers. Did it get more bizarre than this? Well, probably. But I'd rather be pelted with actual snowballs than go through this night again.

I felt Cinderella-like, nearly losing my shoes with every step. If I had glass slippers, they would have frosted over by now.

So far I'd been passed by one car of guys that honked at me and yelled something, and another car of guys that had whistled—either at me, or the little old lady who passed me going the other direction. She'd given me quite a look, like everyone knew that you didn't just walk down Summit on the last night of Winter Carnival in a fancy outfit, as if there were a St. Paul city ordinance against it.

This was shaping up to be one of the worst nights of my life. My teensy-tiny purse wasn't big enough for a cell phone, so I hadn't even been able to call anyone yet.

Beside me, a car pulled over to the curb, and I pulled my jacket more tightly around me. *Leave me alone!* I thought. *Can't you see I'm completely miserable?*

The horn honked but I ignored it. *Maybe I should switch to side streets,* I thought. Fewer cars, less harassment. Or maybe I should find a phone and try calling Gretchen. If I cut over to Grand Avenue, I could probably find a coffee shop or a restaurant that was still open. They'd have to take pity on a poor girl like me. Broken-hearted, and steeped in slush. And without my cell.

I heard the car door slam behind me and kept walking. As I heard footsteps behind me in the wet snow, getting closer and closer, I suddenly got nervous. I glanced over my shoulder.

"We have to stop meeting like this," Conor said.

I just kept walking.

"You know, you on the side of the road, vaguely wandering, me driving past." He jogged a little to catch up to me. "So, nice night. A little snowy, maybe, but it is the theme and all. Kevin's parents probably arranged it somehow."

I laughed, but then stopped myself. "Are you here to rescue me or something?" I asked.

"No. I'm here to see if you want a ride home," Conor said.

"That's what you always say," I complained.

"Hey. I'm all about the rides home," Conor joked.

I turned to him and felt a small smile creep up at the corners of my mouth. "Ha ha."

"Well, it was funny," he said. "Come on, I'll give you a ride home."

"No thanks. I mean, thanks but no thanks," I said, giving him a meaningful look. The last time I'd tried to give him a ride, he'd nearly sprinted away across the parking lot.

"Are we just going to stand here all night quoting each other?" Conor asked. "I mean, not that the material is bad, but I was kind of hoping we could get beyond that."

"Conor! I can't let you give me a ride—"

"Why not?" he interrupted.

"Because—"

"You don't like my truck," he cut in. "I know. It is old, and it is loud, but—"

"No, because—aren't you supposed to be at the party with someone else? You should really get back there," I said. "You completely ditched your date. And even though I really really like you and I'm happy to see you, I just don't think it's very fair to her that you ran out."

"I didn't run out," Conor said. "I sprinted."

"Come on." I pushed him a little bit. "Don't tell me you're the kind of person who'd abandon the person they brought, okay? Because you're not."

"No, I guess not," Conor said with a shrug. He was fighting a smile, but I couldn't figure out why.

"So. Okay. Who is your . . . uh . . . who is she?" I asked.

"The love of my life," Conor said. "What do you think?"

I just stared at him. "Seriously?"

"No, of course not!" Now he playfully shoved

me, for a change. "I mean, I do like her. But that's Janie. We're pals."

"But . . . you came together. Didn't you?"

"What? Oh, no. We ran into each other when we got here. Bumped into her in the entryway."

"Oh." I tried not to smile so much that it hurt, but it was difficult. My mouth kept making this happy shape. It was straining the smile muscles. "Really?" I almost snickered, but I held it back.

"Did you think . . . wow. You thought we were a couple?" Conor asked.

"Well, I asked Sean if you had a date and he said yes," I said.

"Like he knows anything about anyone except himself?" Conor said. "The fact he could remember that he was supposed to pick *you* up is amazing."

"Come on, give him a break," I said. "He's maybe not the best guy . . . but he's not the worst."

"Yeah. Okay. Anyway, do you think that I would ask you out, and then, like, go with someone else?" Conor said.

"I don't know. I mean . . . I was going with Sean, when I really wanted to go with you."

"Aha! I knew it," Conor said.

"And I came to tell you that, and I saw you walk in together, and you were in the corner of that den, talking to her, and I just assumed . . ."

"That we were . . . together together?" Conor laughed. "If you only knew."

I folded my arms in front of me, which wasn't a bad idea anyway because I was getting chilly. "Enlighten me."

"She was upset because she liked someone else there. She was trying to convince me to go talk to him for her."

"You. A matchmaker? Ha. I thought you said you and Janie were good friends. I mean, doesn't she know you better than that?"

"Hey. No fair. I did tell her that asking me to ask someone to dance with her was a little, uh, strange."

"So that's why you were whispering," I said.

"Exactly."

"Hmm." I tapped my shoe against the slushy pavement—a layer of ice had built up underneath the sole so that I couldn't really make contact.

"So. Now what?" Conor asked. He reached

over and pulled some snow out of my hair. "If you don't want a ride home, do you want to go somewhere else?"

I nodded, biting my lip. "Yeah. But where?"

We stood there for a minute, not moving, the snow falling lightly. "I have an idea," Conor said. "Come on." He reached out for my hand. I took it and we headed for the truck.

"See, Gretchen said I was silly to wear this jacket with this dress. But I think you have to admit that it goes very nicely." I smoothed my dress and looked at the way it fanned out over the top of my blue rental skates. "I don't know if I would go with blue, but . . ."

Conor finished tying his hockey skate laces and stood up. "It works," he said.

"Thanks," I said, knowing that I probably looked sort of ridiculous. "How did you know this skating rink was open late?"

We stepped through the opening in the boards onto the ice. A few other people were out, enjoying the evening on skates. Romantic music was playing over a loudspeaker in the corner. The snow had stopped, and the air felt almost warm, with no wind.

"I read about it in the paper," he said. "I knew it was open 'til midnight on the weekends, through February."

"You mean, we can come back?" I asked, looking around at the bright lights of downtown St. Paul, the cathedral up on the hill and the Capitol building.

"That depends," Conor said.

"On what?" I asked.

"Whether you're staying or not." He reached for my hand as we circled the far end of the rink. "And don't shove me when I say this, but I want you to."

"Really?" I asked. "Because I want to, too." I blushed as I heard myself say, "tutu."

Conor's hand was warm and strong. I stuck my right hand into my pocket to keep it warm— I hadn't brought any mittens. In my jacket pocket, though, I felt something woolly. "Ooh! My hat!" I cried.

Conor and I glided to a stop. (Okay, he glided to a stop. Then he stopped *me*.) "Wait. I'll put it on for you," he offered. "I wouldn't want to mess up your hair. It looks really pretty tonight."

"That's the, uh, glitter," I said as Conor took the hat from me. He gently stretched it so that it fit over my head, and he pulled it down to my ears. We stared into each other's eyes for a second. *I'm going to kiss him*, I thought. *I'm totally about to kiss him.*

But then he slid backward a little bit, out of my reach, and took off his scarf. "Here. This will keep you warmer." He came closer again, and looped it around my neck. He pulled both ends into a knot at my neck, and just before he finished I put my hands over his.

He made one final, little tug to pull the scarf tightly, and as he did, my skates slid toward him—and we ended up nose to nose.

"Sorry, I—I'm all out of wool items," Conor stammered as he caught me.

Before he could say anything else, I kissed him. I didn't care that we were in the center of the rink, that we were probably the only people left, that the spotlight might be on us, that the music had stopped and they were about to close. Conor put his hand on my cheek, and gently moved a strand of my hair off to the side as he leaned into the kiss.

Kissing Conor wasn't like anyone else I'd ever kissed before. I could easily have gone weak in the knees, except that I didn't want to fall on the ice in my party dress — not now, anyway. I might miss something.

The spotlights flashed a couple of times, and we broke apart, laughing. "Does that mean they don't approve?" I said, as Conor leaned over and gave me a kiss on the neck.

"Five minutes, people, five minutes," the skate rental person announced over the loudspeaker. "Closing in five minutes."

"Wow. Is it midnight already?" I asked. "We should go. But first . . . what are you doing on Thursday?" I asked as we started skating over to the benches.

"I don't know," Conor said. "I think I have to work."

"Well, too bad, because you're coming away with me."

"Oh, really?"

"Really," I said. "Please?"

"Oh, okay. If I have to. But wait. Am I just going to show up some old boyfriend or something?"

"No. Of course not."

"Too bad, because I could really get into that."

"Well, whatever suits you," I said. As I was stepping off the ice, I stopped for a second and leaned back against him. He kissed the back of my neck, but surprisingly, it didn't freeze on contact.

"You know what? You're shivering," he said as he wrapped his arms more tightly around me, trying to keep me warm.

I wasn't sure whether it was from the cold, or from what had just happened. "I think my toes got a little frozen, that's all," I said.

"I know a place we can go where it's really warm," Conor said. "The bakery."

I couldn't get those silly blue rental skates off fast enough. Besides, they really did kill my outfit.

Chapter 20

$\mathcal{I}$ tiptoed into the house, holding my stiletto-heeled shoes, and wearing Conor's wool socks over my stockings. I was carrying a little bag from the bakery, with a few donuts for Brett.

I closed the door as quietly as I could. I was hoping I could sneak upstairs—Gretchen would no doubt have gone to sleep hours ago.

But when I turned around, I saw a light on in the kitchen, and both Sean and Gretchen— even on crutches—jumped up when they saw me.

Bear started to bark when he saw me, and he raced and jumped on me, nearly knocking me over. I dropped the bag of donuts and he was on top of that immediately, but I managed to get them away from him.

"Is Brett up, too?" I joked as I shrugged out of my jacket.

"No, he's asleep, but we stayed up half the night worrying about you!" Gretchen said.

"What?" I asked.

"I was worried sick about you," she said. She stared at the socks on my feet. I hoped she wouldn't ask me about them. I noticed tear stains on her cheeks and felt this sudden stab of very, very intense guilt. You always called. That was our parents' mantra.

"So was I," Sean said. "Are you okay?"

I laughed, trying to break the tension. "You were worried? I'm sorry."

"It's not funny, Kirsten." Gretchen sank back down at the kitchen table. "You should have called."

"Yes. Okay, I probably should have," I said to Gretchen. "But I didn't bring my phone. It wouldn't fit into my purse, remember?"

"Well, I figured that out after I called it five times and I kept hearing this ringing coming from your room," she said angrily. "How could you not bring your phone?"

"You're the one who told me I wouldn't need

it—you're the one who said I should bring this itty-bitty useless purse." I slammed it down on the counter. Why was she treating me like a twelve-year-old?

"I'm responsible for you when you're here," she said. "if you didn't make it home, I'd have to call Mom and Dad and tell them you were missing, and—"

"Gretchen, don't you know me well enough to know I can take care of myself?" I asked.

"Someone told me you ran out of the party by yourself. Why did you do that?" Sean asked. "I kept trying to find you."

"I'm sorry, Sean. Really. I left because . . . I just wasn't having a very good time. And you were, and I didn't want to ruin that, so . . ."

"How did you get here? Did you walk all the way?" Sean asked. "That's like ten miles."

So he hadn't noticed that Conor and I left at the same time. Didn't he have a clue that the only other person I really knew here was Conor? He could be so slow sometimes.

"Actually, Sean . . . I know this is going to sound bad. And I don't want to hurt your feelings or anything," I said. "But Conor and I sort of, well, took off together. He gave me a ride home."

"Are you *serious*?" Gretchen screamed, pounding the table with her fist.

"Shh! Brett's sleeping. Anyway, what? I thought you'd be glad I was safe," I said.

"Wait a second. You and Conor?" Sean looked a little exhausted, as he stood under the fluorescent overhead light, his tie hanging loosely from his collar, his suit jacket unbuttoned. "Since when?"

"Since . . . I don't know," I said. "Tonight?"

"Oh." Sean sighed. "Well, I just wish you'd told me. I spent half the night looking for you."

"I'm sorry," I said. "That was really thoughtless of me. You're right, and I'm sorry, really."

He looked at me for a second and then shrugged. "Whatever. I'm too tired to deal with it right now. See you guys."

I hurried after him to the front door. "Sean, I'm sorry," I said again. "I hope I didn't ruin the night. I mean, it seemed like you were having fun and everything."

"Yeah, it was okay. There'll be another party

soon anyway." He gave me a half-smile, then walked out the door, and I watched him start jogging up the block toward his house.

When I turned around, Gretchen was sitting on the living room sofa, waiting for me. Her body language and tone of voice said it clearly: *I hate you right now.* "Since when are you interested in Conor?"

"Since . . . a while ago. I mean, not that long, but he really, I don't know, grew on me, I guess you could say. I kind of just figured it out myself," I admitted as I sat across from her.

"Does everyone else know?" she asked.

"No. Why would you ask that?"

"Because! You tell your friends more than you tell me. You always have," she said in a hurt tone.

"They don't know either, okay? It's private," I said. "I don't want to talk about everything with everyone. Some things should be private."

She buried her face in her hands. "Private. That means you're having sex, that's why you didn't come home until two in the morning—"

I felt like throwing a magazine from her

cutesy wood magazine rack at her. "No, it doesn't! That's not me at all. You don't even know me."

"I do," she said. "And that's why I think you should really consider staying with Sean."

"What? Are you crazy?"

"No. And I resent that. I think I know a little more about guys and relationships than you do, Kirsten."

"Okay, *Mom*," I said. "Spill. Tell me your wisdom."

"I think things could really work out with you and Sean. He's a great guy—"

"So is Conor," I interrupted. "Do you know how many nice things Conor has done since I got here?" I told her about the times he'd made sure I was okay. I left out the bit about insulting me and running over my foot with a grocery cart.

"So he likes to follow you around," she said. "Does that prove anything?"

"Yes. Actually, it does," I said. "You don't know Conor. You said so yourself."

"But what's wrong with Sean? And how could you just ditch him at that party? He asked you to go with him, and you run out with his brother?"

"It wasn't like that," I said.

"I bet."

"Honestly! First of all, Sean and I were already, like, running on fumes. We didn't have anything in common. And once we hit the party, that was so obvious. He kept hanging out with his pals, and these other girls—we danced together like twice."

"He said you had a nice time, until you vanished," Gretchen said.

"So you've never known two people to have different versions of the same events?" I just stared at her. "Sean barely knew I was there. But that was okay! Maybe I was keeping my distance, too, maybe that was part of the problem. Because I'd realized I wanted to be with Conor."

"You went about it all wrong," Gretchen said. "You made a mess of everything. And I don't understand why you wouldn't just break your date with Sean if—"

"I know, I probably should have," I said. "In retrospect. But at the time, I felt like I had to go through with it. Sean was counting on me, *you* were counting on me—"

"So now it's my fault?" She shook her head. "Kirsten, you have a lot to learn about maturity."

"So do you," I shot back. "You sit around here doing nothing but telling me how to run my life and how I should look and what I should wear and who I should date. You know, I'm really sorry about your divorce and I'm sorry about your leg, but that doesn't give you the right to tell me how to live my life, okay? 'Cause I don't really admire the way you live yours. So why don't you focus on your own for a change?"

I took a deep breath after all the words came out. I guess I'd been saving them up for a while.

Gretchen practically snorted. "You don't know anything. The reason I'm so mad about staying up late tonight is that I have an interview tomorrow and I'm going to look like—like—crap, thanks to you!"

"What?" I asked quietly, still feeling guilty about my mini-tirade.

"I have an interview. For a job. It's a second interview, actually," she said.

"No way." I started to laugh a little. Everything was out in the open now, and we were still talking. "Really? That's so cool."

"I don't know." She rubbed her cast with her wrist. "Do you think I can handle it after all this time off?"

"Gretchen. You can handle anything," I said. "I've been watching you handle stuff since, you know. Forever."

"Yeah?"

"Yes. So tell me about it," I urged.

"Well. Since you got here, I've been doing a lot. You probably didn't notice, you were either too busy with Brett, or out with those guys. Maybe you were really focused on yourself, not me," she said. "Did you ever think of that?"

I shrank down in my chair. She had a point. Whenever I focused on Gretchen, it was to find fault with her constant shop & spend & sofa mode.

"Anyway, first I went to a career counselor, and I found out what I really wanted to do."

"You did? When?"

"The first week when you were here. I asked you to drop me at the doctor?" she reminded me. "And all those mornings that you went to the bakery, I was doing online job hunting, while Brett watched 'Sesame Street.' And whenever you took Brett places? I tried to do phone interviews, and work on my resume, send out letters and stuff."

"So, wait a second. You've been doing all this over the past month while I've been here? Seriously?" I asked. "What's the interview for? Is it a job you really want?"

She nodded, and smiled. "It's retail management."

"What else," I said. "Of course that makes sense!"

"That day we went to the Mall of America, and you took Brett to Camp Snoopy, I went to a few stores. It wasn't easy on crutches, but I managed," she said. "Anyway, this would be to roll out and manage a new store, at a different mall."

I just sat there, not knowing whether to laugh or cry. It made complete sense: The woman who was born to shop and spend would now help others do the same thing. And she was great at it, and now she'd get paid for it. And I'd helped, even though I didn't know about it. *But, wait a second,* I thought. "Did Mom know about this?" I asked.

"Yes. It was her idea that having you here might help me get around to doing the job search. She said she'd give me a month to get my act together." Gretchen leaned back on the sofa and sighed. "She was very un-Mom-like. She didn't say anything about things working out— she said the only way to make that happen was to work them out myself."

"But . . . you did break your leg, right? Or was that fake?" I asked.

"Of course I did!" She laughed. "But it's not as bad as they thought. It should be okay in another couple of weeks. Then if I can just find a daycare that will work with my hours."

"I'll stick around until you do," I said.

"But don't you need to get back home?"

"Yes. And no," I said. "We can work something out."

"You are the best. Even if your waltzing

321

sucks. And your taste in boys is questionable at best. And you're only staying so you can be with Conor."

"That's not the *only* reason," I said. "You know that, right?"

"I think so." She smiled. "Now what did you bring home in that bakery bag, because I could go for something sweet."

"You wouldn't like it," I said.

"I'll be the judge of that," she said.

"Okay, fine." Before I went into the kitchen, I leaned down and gave Gretchen a hug. "I'm really proud of you. I'm sorry you were worried tonight."

"It's okay." She hugged me back. "I'm sorry I've been a pain lately. Now *run*."

Chapter 21

When I got up Thursday morning and looked outside to check the weather for our trip up north, I saw Sean sitting on the front steps. Maybe it was a mirage, I told myself as I looked again. I hadn't slept much the night before, because I was so excited about the trip.

What was he doing here? This was awkward. Was his shovel broken or something? Or was he here to tell me that Conor couldn't go away with me—that he and I were back on instead?

I opened the front door a crack. "So, did it snow?" I asked him.

"Oh, hey, Kirsten." He glanced over his shoulder at me. He had dark circles under his eyes, as if he hadn't slept all that well either. "Good morning."

"What's up?" I asked. "Are you okay?"

He got to his feet. "Yeah. I'm fine."

"Well, do you need something?" He wasn't here to try and win me back or something romantic like that, was he? He had this serious, distressed look on his face, his forehead semi-creased with worry.

"I just wanted to talk to you for a minute," he said. "Do you have time?"

"Clearly," I said. I was standing there in my sweats, having decided to sleep in clothes that might not always look like pajamas from now on. "Do you want to come in?"

"Could we sit out here?" Sean asked. "I don't really want to see Gretchen or Brett, if that's okay."

"That's cool. I'll be right out," I said. I grabbed my jacket from the hook on the closet door and put on my boots. Looking at them reminded me of the Snow White costume. Hopefully Sean wouldn't have the same memory.

I grabbed my mittens and went outside. Sean was sitting on the porch swing, so I went over to sit beside him.

"First of all, I want to apologize," Sean said.

"No! I should be the one apologizing," I said. "I know I should have been honest with you, when I felt like I was kind of, I don't know. Like maybe Conor and I had more in common and . . . I just really liked you and I'd already said I'd go to the dance and the cabin with you, so . . ."

Ugh, listen to me, I thought. I was sounding a lot like Emma Dilemma. I love the girl, but I didn't want to emulate her dating style. "Anyway. I'm sorry if I was rude at the party, or worried you that night, or any of that," I said.

"I'm sorry, too," Sean said. "I was just . . . I liked you and everything. I mean, you showed up here in town and you're funny and cute, I thought, well, I just wanted to hang out with you. And then I saw that Conor liked you, and when I realized there were like a hundred reasons to like you . . . I felt like I had to go out with you, instead of him."

We sat there, swinging back and forth for a minute. I wondered if he felt as stupid about this as I did. There was no reason we couldn't go out with each other, but there was no reason we should, either. We just didn't have that intense connection, the way you should if you're going to spend that much time with someone and, like, make out with him.

"I guess what I want to say is that, despite everything that's happened, I really like you," Sean said.

I stopped swinging. What?

"That's why I have to tell you something. It's really, really important."

"Okay . . ." I said slowly.

"As much as we argue, and fight, and criticize each other? Conor's a really good guy. You can trust him."

I let out a sigh of relief. "Yeah?" I asked.

"Yeah. For sure." He nodded. "But if it turns out you can't? And he's awful to you? You know where I live."

I laughed. "Are you seriously going to be that nice to me?"

"Sure. Why not?"

"I think you're too nice," I said. "That's why you have all those girls around you all the time. You have to be a little, you know, discriminating or something. Be mean to a few of 'em. Thin the pack."

"Thin the pack? What am I, a wolf now?" Sean slid off the swing and caught the chain to keep it from whacking me. "I know we act like jerks to each other, but he's still my brother. I'd stick up for him over anybody. Even when he does stupid things like walking out on a team."

"Yeah, I know what you mean." I thought about Gretchen and our argument the night before. Maybe we'd never be that much alike, but I'd knock down any guy—anyone, period—who tried to hurt her.

"Aunt Kirsten likes boys, Aunt Kirsten likes Sean . . ."

"Conor," I tried to correct Brett for the umpteenth time.

The four—make that five, counting Bear—of us were standing outside by Conor's pickup. A light snow was falling, and we'd just spent the required five minutes discussing the weather as we prepared to take off for the Groundhog weekend.

Gretchen had tried to give me some advice over breakfast, in terms of how far to go with

Conor on our first weekend away together. I told her that one, I didn't plan on sleeping with him or any guy until I was older, and two, we'd be sleeping in a cabin with a bunch of other people, so not to worry. That seemed to put her mind at ease.

"Don't break your leg," she said to me.

"I won't!" I said. "Will you quit saying that already?"

All of a sudden, Brett stopped chanting my name, and got this big lower lip as I opened the passenger door to the rusty pickup truck. His eyes filled with tears and he started to cry.

I crouched down, wrapped my arms around him and gave him a big hug. "I'll be back soon. I promise."

"You'd better be," Gretchen said. "I need a driver." Then she smiled. "And a friend."

We gave each other a quick hug, and then I climbed into the pickup beside Conor.

Gretchen leaned into his window. "Take care of her."

"Got it," he said.

"And drive really carefully."

"No problem. It's a light snow. I think it'll taper off soon."

"Okay, bye!" I called out as we pulled away from the curb. "Man," I sighed. "I thought we'd never get out of there. Could you and Gretchen talk about cold fronts any longer?"

"Well, what else are we supposed to talk about?" Conor said. "Uh oh. I think we've got a problem." He kept glancing in the rearview mirror. "Look behind us."

I was afraid to look. I figured it must be Gretchen waving her arms, yelling "Stop! Stop!"

But when I finally turned around, I saw Bear. He was running at top speed, like an Iditarod sled dog competitor, bounding along the middle of the street after us.

"Loyal, isn't he?" Conor remarked as we slowed to a stop.

By the time we got Bear back home and got on the highway, the snow had started coming down harder. Then it fell even more heavily. After a while, we were going so slowly due to ice buildup, and lack of visibility, that we had only made it about ten miles in an hour.

"This has kind of turned into a blizzard," I commented. "Did we even hit St. Paul yet?"

Conor laughed. "Yeah. We're about fifty miles out of town."

"We're actually not going to make it to the cabin. Are we?"

"No. I don't think so."

I started laughing. After all that. After everything I'd gone through to get a date for this silly weekend, after all the money I'd spent, the risky deposit for two. Now we weren't even going to get there.

"I think we should pull over here," Conor said as he peered at the exit sign in the distance. "It's only getting worse. We can sit for a while and see if the storm's going to stop."

We made it to a SuperAmerica gas station, where several other cars had pulled in to assess the situation. I went inside to buy us a few sodas and asked the clerk what the roads looked like, going north. "They've got a foot already in Duluth," she said. "Lots of cars are stuck, and there's this real icy section where people are going off the road, near Hinckley."

That did not sound good. I pulled out my cell phone and called Jones, but she didn't answer. I hoped she'd made it okay. I left her a message, then called Emma. She was already at the cabin with Donny, her latest, and Crystal and Eric were there with them. They had had a much shorter drive to the cabin, and they'd left home before the storm, so they were already settled in, sitting by the fire and watching the snow come down.

"Kirsten, it's okay, you can admit it," Emma said. "You didn't find a date for the weekend. Come on up anyway."

"I'm serious!" I said. "We're stranded." I looked out at Conor, who was scraping the ice off the windshield because the truck's aging defroster was overwhelmed.

"Wait—here's Jones! Hey, you made it!" I heard everyone laughing and talking, and then Jones picked up the phone.

"Where are you, Kirst?"

"We're trying to get there, but the roads are awful," I said.

"You are cursed, Kirst. You realize that."

"I know. We're going to stay here for a while

until it stops snowing and sleeting and whatever else. Hopefully we'll make it later tonight,
or else tomorrow."

"You and . . . ?"

Just then, Conor walked into the store,
shaking the snow off his jacket.

I'd kept the secret this long. Why not a few
more hours? "See you tomorrow, for sure.
Okay?" I said to Jones. "Bye!"

Conor and I left the gas station shop and ran
to the pickup truck. Just before we got in, I
made a snowball and quickly tossed it at him. It
was the perfect snow for making snowballs—
wet, heavy and easy to clump together. We circled the truck, and the gas pumps, hiding out,
tossing them at each other. Soon other people
got out of their cars and joined in—soon the
entire gas station was filled with people hiding
behind their cars and pelting whoever dared
come out from behind their car to walk into the
shop.

We were laughing so hard when we finally
got back into the truck to warm up. "Well.
Should we settle in for the night, or what?"
Conor asked.

"I guess so," I said with a shrug.

We had our sleeping bags in the back, under the truck cap, and Conor made a little nest with blankets and some of our clothes.

We climbed in together, and snuggled up close. As I was lying there, trying to fall asleep, I scraped a little part of frost off the window. **K + C**, I traced with my fingernail. Then I drew a heart around it.

"Are you seeing things again? Hearts in the ice? Like you saw hearts in your lattes?" Conor teased me.

"Did you, or did you not, intentionally make a pattern in my coffee that morning?"

"I did not," Conor said. "But I take full credit for it anyway."

"That is so like you!" I giggled as Conor pulled me over toward him, taking a chunk of snow out of my hair.

"I can't believe we're spending the night in the truck," Conor said. "I've never done something like this before. Well, except for the time I ran away from home."

"When was that?"

"When I was sixteen. I got so mad at everyone

that I just left, you know? The problem was, I forgot the sleeping bag and blankets part." He snuggled closer. "It was February."

"You went home. End of story," I said.

"No, I made a snow mattress," Conor said. "You know, the way animals do? If you lie on the snow it's really warm."

"Okay," I said slowly. "I think I'm just going to take your word on that. For a change." I turned slightly so that I was lying on my back. "Though it would be cool to lie outside and look at the stars right now."

"Yeah, but it's still snowing," Conor said. He turned over, too, and we laid side by side, holding hands. "So . . . what's it going to be like tomorrow?"

"We'll have to see, I guess," I said.

And then I fell asleep, cuddled next to Conor, completely toasty warm in the cold truck in the middle of a snowstorm.

Chapter 22

"You made it!"

"Kirst!"

"She's here!"

Everyone screamed as Emma opened the door and Conor and I walked into the log cabin—which was actually more like a big lodge—the next morning.

Well, maybe not everyone, maybe just the girls shrieked. In any case, I felt like a celebrity.

Emma, Jones, Keira and Crystal all gathered around me in a hug. "That's not Sean," Jones whispered in my right ear, as Emma said, "Isn't that goalie guy?" in my left.

I cleared my throat as we separated and said, "Conor, this is everyone. Everyone, this is Conor."

Fortunately, nobody gasped. At least not that I heard.

Tyler and I exchanged polite nods in greeting, and I said hi to Emma and Crystal's boyfriends, Donny and Eric. It looked like Jones had come by herself. I admired her for that. Not that I wanted to trade places with her right now, because I was very happy I'd brought Conor along. Maybe I'd started off with the wrong intentions—finding a guy just to bring here—but I'd ended up with something—someone—great.

"Oh, no!" Crystal suddenly cried, and she rushed back to the large, open kitchen. I thought I saw a little smoke coming from the stove, but I ignored it as we sat down on the rustic furniture by the fireplace.

Keira brought each of us a mug of coffee, and everyone gathered around to hear about our trip.

"It's so great you could finally make it," Emma said. "Were you scared?"

"Us? No." Conor shook his head. "Kirsten might have scared some people at the gas station when she started whipping snowballs at them, but—"

"You did what?" Tyler asked.

"It was boring. It's called letting off tension," I said.

Crystal came over with a big plate, stacked high with pancakes. "Help yourselves, okay? A couple of these are sort of burned, sorry," she said. "That stove is weird. All of a sudden it gets really hot."

We all loaded up some breakfast onto paper plates and sat back down to eat.

"Yum. We're going to need this energy for when we go skiing—"

"And snowshoeing—"

"And hiking—"

"I don't know if I should have maple syrup, or jam," Emma said, tapping her knife against the table. "What do you guys think? I love syrup, but that raspberry jam looks really good."

Jones looked at me and rolled her eyes. "Emma Dilemma. Have both. Okay? Just have both."

We both cracked up laughing, and I saw Conor giving me a confused look out of the corner of my eye. Then I turned to him and saw that he wasn't confused; he was trying to choke down one of the burned pancakes, and he seemed to be struggling.

"Fear factor: pancake edition," he mumbled to me after he'd managed to swallow the bite.

Together we managed through our laughter to hide his plate under mine, and we shared the less-done pancake. Which, when you got to the center of it, turned out to be a little raw.

Luckily, we'd bought some donuts at the gas station — they were selling them for a quarter to everyone who'd camped out for the night, and we had sort of a party with coffee in the parking lot as everyone got ready to move on.

"No matter what? We'll always have SuperAmerica," Conor had said as we pulled out onto the highway.

"Oh, yes," I said, laughing as I checked out the photos on my cell phone. "Isn't that romantic?"

"I guess I picked up a few things from the pigeon scout," Jones said that night. She'd just managed to start a fire outside, on the snowy beach at the edge of the large lake where the cabin was located. We were right in the middle of the woods—it was completely deserted, except for a few other big log cabins nearby. No one else was having a bonfire that night.

"Did you guys hear? The groundhog saw its shadow this morning. You know what that means," Crystal said.

"Six more weeks of winter," I said. We'd spent the day cross-country skiing, snow shoeing and hanging out. Everyone seemed to approve of Conor—though they were still confused about what had happened with Sean. I'd fill them in later, when we had a chance to talk, just the four of us.

"We live in Minnesota. Like we didn't know that we had six more weeks of winter already," Jones said. "More like a *hundred*, probably."

Crystal groaned. "Don't remind me, okay?"

"You need a spring break trip," I said. "In fact, maybe we all do . . . right?"

"You think maybe you could spend six more weeks in Minneapolis?" Conor asked me.

"Well, Gretchen is really not all better," I said. "I mean, clearly. Plus, I told her I'd help her get started in her new job."

I thought of how worried she was when I

got home, and how we'd had that big fight and made up and felt tears welling·in my eyes. I'd called her several times already since we'd been gone, just to let her know I was okay.

"You know that movie, *Groundhog Day*? Maybe we could live through this day over and over," Conor said as I leaned against him.

"Yeah, but then we'd have to eat Crystal's pancakes of lead again," I whispered to him.

He rubbed his stomach and said softly, "I think I'll take over the baking tomorrow." I nodded.

I looked around the fire at everyone, taking stock of my friends and their significant others.

Crystal and Eric were solid—they'd been together for a year plus. On the other side of the fire, I knew Emma wouldn't stay with Donny. And I knew Keira and Tyler would barely make it through the weekend, because Tyler was still staring at Emma. He clearly only kept dating her friends so he could be around her.

For some reason, I had a feeling Conor and I would be together next Groundhog Day.

"Come on," I said. I stood up and held out

my hand to him. "Let's go to the middle of the lake."

"Right now?" he asked. "But the fire—"

"Just for a sec," I said.

"This isn't some trick where you're going to pelt me with snowballs again, is it?" he asked. "Or shove me on the ice?"

"Come *on*!" I cried.

We ran to the middle of the lake, laid down in the snow, and made snow angels looking up at the starry sky. When you're so far out in the country, it feels like you can see a million stars.

"You know how you accused me of seeing stuff, at the bakery. Like, hearts, and smiles? I . . . well, I made a pattern of my own for you." I got to my feet and fished a flashlight out of my pocket. "It got dark before I was done, so I couldn't show you before, and if it snows tonight, it might cover it up, so . . ."

Conor stood up and held out his hand for the flashlight. "Give."

I slapped it into his palm and waited while he switched it on. The stars were so bright, I could almost read the giant letters I'd tracked into the snow without the flashlight.

I ♥ U CONOR.

"All those instant messages you've been writing are really paying off. You've been working on your abbreviations," Conor teased me. "What school do you go to again?"

I started chasing him across the lake. "It's a very good school. *Very!*"

For more snow-covered fun, turn the page to check out

Love on the Lifts
BY RACHEL HAWTHORNE

Warning: beginners may fall
head-over-heels!

$\mathcal{A}$ totally hot ski instructor," Leah suddenly announced excitedly. "That's what you need to take your mind completely off Brad Connor."

"How can a ski instructor be *hot*?" I asked. "His classroom is a snow-covered hill. He's gotta be cold."

Allie rolled her eyes and Leah gave me a sharp look that said she was seriously contemplating throwing the snow she'd just scooped up at me.

"That is so lame, Kate."

Okay, so it *was* lame, but I was also extremely cold, with visions of curling up in front of a roaring fire dancing through my head. And obviously, the chill seeping through the knitted cap I'd pulled down over my ears was causing periodic brain freezes. Even stuffing my shoulder-length, obnoxiously naturally curly red hair under the cap didn't seem to provide any extra insulation against the frigid air that surrounded us.

And it was unbelievably cold. After all, we were in a ski resort town with white peaked mountains all around us.

Leah, Allie, and I had flown in earlier that afternoon. My aunt had met us at the airport and driven us to Snow Angel Valley where she'd made arrangements for us to stay in a condo by ourselves. It was totally awesome. Three bedrooms, a sunken living room, a red-wood deck. But more importantly, it was ours for the duration of our visit. Just ours. No parents, no chaperones. We were totally on our own, with the freedom to do exactly what we wanted.

Once we'd settled into our respective bedrooms, Allie had announced that she wanted to build a snowman. But now that we were actually doing it, the activity seemed as lame as my joke. I mean, really, we were seniors, and a snowman is something you care about if you're, like, two years old—or if you've never been around snow.

Leah and Allie had never been around snow.

I saw it at least once a year, usually over winter break when I came to visit Aunt Sue while my parents took their annual gotta-get-away-from-it-all cruise down to the Bahamas. Aunt Sue lived in Snow Angel Valley, owned a bookstore-slash-hot chocolate café, and rented condos to the tourists more than she did to the locals. This winter break, remarkably, one of her condos wasn't being rented.

She is absolutely, without question, one of the coolest people I know. Especially since she told me that I could bring along a couple of my friends to share the condo with me.

So I did. Leah Locke and Allie Anderson. And I'm Kate Kennedy. We call ourselves the alphabet trio because somehow we all ended up with our first and last names starting with the same letter. Alliteration. Of course, we have a lot more in common than our alliterating names.

We attend the same high school, live in the same neighborhood, have the same best friends (each other), and are presently boyfriendless.

Although I have to admit that I've been crushing on my brother's college roommate Brad Connor ever since Mom, Dad, and I went to the university to visit Sam during family weekend. That's when I met Brad. And oh my gosh, is he a hunk. Tall, dark, and handsome doesn't even begin to describe him. He has a killer smile—

"Why are we making our snowman round?" Leah asked, interrupting my nostalgic musings about Brad.

"Because that's the way snowmen are supposed to be," Allie said.

"How would you know how snowmen are supposed to be?" Leah asked.

"I've seen pictures," Allie retorted.

The part of Texas where we live had never been visited by a single snowflake, which was the reason they were so totally into building this snow guy.

Leah picked up a twig. "Let's be creative. Let's make him buff, give him some abs, some guns—"

"Guns? Are you going to make him a cowboy—" I began.

"No." Leah held her arm up at a right angle, closing her hand into a fist. "Guns. Muscled arms. That's what my brother calls them."

"Guess I don't know about guns, since Sam isn't into that whole being-in-shape thing. He's so incredibly skinny."

"He's not that skinny," Allie said.

"He's not buff, either."

"But our snowman should be," Leah said. "Otherwise, he's like everyone else's snowman, and what fun is that? Come on, let's put him on a diet and into a workout program."

She knelt in front of our lopsided snowman. He was really pitiful-looking, listing to the side a bit, all lumpy, not at all the way snowmen appeared in drawings that I'd seen in picture books when I was a kid.

"I think we can turn him into a sexy stud," Leah said.

"*You* can turn him into a sexy stud. I'm pretty sure I hear hot chocolate calling to me." Aunt Sue's shop had more than fifty varieties and was only a couple of blocks up the street.

"It won't take me that long. Let me finish before it gets dark. Tomorrow we'll be skiing and I might not be able to get back to him."

"I don't think he's going to melt anytime soon."

"I like to finish what I start."

That was true enough. I'd never known anyone as single-minded as Leah. I couldn't deny my best friend this one small pleasure. Besides, like I said, she'd never been around snow. I wanted her to enjoy it as much as possible.

"Not a problem. The hot chocolate will wait," I told her, as I sat on the wooden steps that led up to the redwood deck.

The condo was situated on a hill, sloping down into the back. The lower level, what I considered the basement, wasn't completely underground. It had high windows that actually looked out on the backyard. From the street, we'd entered the second level of the house, which was considered the main area and contained the sunken living room, a kitchen, and a bedroom. If we walked through the main room, we came to the sliding glass doors that led out to

6

the deck, where water from the hot tub steamed up to create a foggy mist.

Why anyone would need a hot tub during the winter was beyond me, but there you have it. All the condos on this street had steam rising from hot tubs. I had yet to see anyone use one. A waste of electricity keeping the water heated, as far as I was concerned.

We'd gone through the sliding glass door and down the steps to play in the backyard. To build our snowman. Like little kids.

So much snow had fallen before we got here that our booted feet sunk into it when we walked over the ground. It covered the deck and the steps. Which was good. You want lots of snow—powder—when you're going skiing.

I tucked my gloved hands into the pockets of my parka and watched as Leah began scraping away some of the snow that we'd worked so hard to gather up for our creation.

She stopped and glanced over her shoulder. "So what do you think about what I said? Let's find you a ski instructor."

There was that single-minded purpose of hers.

Both Leah and Allie, by virtue of being my best friends, knew about my crush. They also knew that he looked through me like I was an open window.

I wrinkled my cold nose. At least I think I wrinkled it. It was frigid, almost numb. "I don't know. I really like Brad. Going after a ski instructor seems a little bit like being unfaithful."

"But he hardly knows you exist," Leah pointed out.

"True, but a ski instructor would be temporary—"

"Which is why he would be so perfect. No long-term commitment. Just short-term fun!"

"I think Leah's idea is fantastic!" Allie exclaimed. "We spend the time while we're here honing our flirtation skills. Then when you tell your brother that each of us was heavily involved with someone over winter break—"

"Why would I tell Sam that *all* of us were involved with someone?"

Looking down, Allie stomped the toe of her white boot against the snow, creating a hole. "I don't know. He might want to know what all of us did. Or you could just tell him about your experiences. My point being"—she lifted her gaze back to mine—"that when Sam tells Brad that you had a guy chasing after you, Brad's interest will skyrocket and he'll be all about getting to know you."

"Do you really think that Sam—not knowing that I have a crush on Brad—is going to tell Brad anything at all about what I do? Guys are not like girls. They talk about dumb stuff, like who is the best NFL quarterback and where can they find a handy poker tournament. They don't try to figure out how they can get together with someone."

"Maybe you should tell Sam how you feel about his roommate," Allie said. "Maybe he'd invite Brad to come home with him on the weekends."

"Right. Like Sam is going to care. He thinks I'm just his stupid baby sister."

"You think he's your stupid older brother, so it all works out," Leah said, backing up a little to inspect the snowman's abs.

I had to admit he was starting to look pretty good. Not a surprise really. Leah is heavy into art, and sculpting is her thing. That and designing tattoos.

"Because he *is* stupid," I said, responding to her comment about Sam. "He treats me like a kid, even though he's only a year older than me."

"But he's in college—" Allie began.

"So? I'll be in college next year. Besides, he's always treated me like I'm just a kid. I can't tell him anything personal or important. I especially can't tell him anything like 'I think your roommate is God's gift to girls.' He'd make my life impossible."

"Brad *is* cute," Leah said.

Under the pretense of wanting to record the history of my brother's year at college, I'd asked to take a picture of Sam with his roommate. Unfortunately, the zoom on my digital camera had somehow been pressed—by a renegade finger, I assumed—and I'd only been able to get a really good close-up shot of Brad. No evidence of Sam in sight. Gosh, darn. What a shame!

The photo was now the background wallpaper on my computer desktop.

"His eyes are so incredibly blue. It's like

looking into a vast sky." I sighed. "I could look into them all day, all night."

"His whole package is good-looking," Leah said. "Kinda like our snowman now."

I smiled. "He is looking good."

"Are you talking about the snowman or Brad?"

"Both." She'd given the snowman abs, a chest, and upper arms—guns.

Leah tossed aside his rock eyes and his pencil nose—we hadn't been able to find a carrot. Aunt Sue had stocked the fridge and pantry for us, but she obviously hadn't expected us to undertake creating a snowman, us being seniors and all. Hence, no carrot.

"Who should I make him look like?" Leah asked.

"Kate's Brad," Allie said.

"He's not my Brad."

"He could be if you'd practice on a ski instructor," Leah said.

"I don't know. It sounds so . . . tawdry."

"And that's a problem because . . ."

She left the question dangling on the air,

waiting for me to come up with a good excuse.

"Look, it doesn't hurt to kiss a few frogs before finally kissing your prince," she added, tired of waiting for me.

"Are you going to flirt with a ski instructor?" I asked.

"You bet."

I looked at Allie. "Are you?"

It was difficult to tell because she was so bundled up but I think she shrugged. "I guess. What can it hurt? Besides, I could use a little romance in my life."

"I think we all can," Leah said. "After all, we'll be here for three whole weeks. We might as well have someone hot to cuddle against and keep us warm."

"All right. I'm game if y'all are," I said. I didn't want to be the only one without someone to snuggle with.

"Great!" Leah pointed her gloved finger at our buff snowman. "Okay, back to the really important issue. Who should I make him look like?"

Leah is like that. Carrying on two or three

conversations at once. Sometimes she makes my head spin.

"Well, if Kate doesn't want it to be Brad, how about Colin Farrell," Allie suggested.

"All right. Let's pack some more snow on his head so I have enough to work with," Leah instructed.

Reaching down I scooped up a handful of snow. I shoved myself up from the steps, walked over to the snowman, and patted the snow into the ball on top of his body.

"I've seen some pictures of awesome ice sculptures," I said. "In Alaska or somewhere. Every year they create all these fantastic sculptures."

"I'd love to do something like that," Leah said. "Maybe I'll create a garden of snow sculptures while I'm here."

"Well, you have plenty of snow to work with." I glanced off into the distance. The mountains were beautiful, covered in glistening white.

"We'll be on the mountains tomorrow," I told them. "I can't wait."

A snowball unexpectedly and painfully

pounded hard into the back of my head. "Ow!"

Putting my hand back there, rubbing the sore spot, I spun around and could hardly believe my eyes. My irksome brother was standing on the wooden deck, a huge cocky grin plastered on his irritatingly handsome face.

Why had I gotten stuck with the red hair and freckles like Mom while he had not a freckle in sight and had inherited Dad's dark hair? I tried to take consolation in the fact that he wouldn't hold on to that beautiful thick hair forever. Eventually, hopefully, it would start to disappear like Dad's was now doing.

"You're building a snowman? What are you, like, two years old?" he taunted.

I was stunned. My brain wouldn't function, no words would come forth. Because standing right beside him, grinning as well, was . . .

Brad Connor.

Also by Catherine Clark . . .

Pb 0-06-056725-2

Hc 0-06-009070-7
Pb 0-06-0447385-6

Hc 0-06-055980-2
Pb 0-06-055982-9

Pb 0-380-81443-9

Maine Squeeze
Colleen's summer looks great: new job, new boyfriend, and no parents (they're in Europe!). It's perfect, until last summer's boyfriend shows up and things get complicated. . . .

Frozen Rodeo
Her mom's pregnant, her dad is staging a professional ice-skating comeback, and her summer school teacher is insane—welcome to Peggy Fleming Farrell's crazy summer!

The Alison Rules
Alison has a lot of rules. But when charming Patrick moves into town, she realizes that no matter how many rules you have, life still happens to you.

Truth or Dairy
Courtney's humiliated, angry, and through with boys! Or at least that's what she says . . .

AVON BOOKS
An Imprint of HarperCollinsPublishers

HarperCollinsPublishers
www.catherineclark.com